Pretty Boy Detective Club

The Dark Star that Shines for You Alone

By NISIOISIN

Translated by Winifred Bird

VERTICAL.

Pretty Boy Detective Club
The Dark Star that Shines for You Alone

Editor: Daniel Joseph

BISHOUNEN TANTEIDAN
KIMI DAKE NI HIKARI KAGAYAKU ANKOKUSEI

© 2015 NISIOISIN

All rights reserved.

First published in Japan in 2015
by Kodansha Ltd., Tokyo.

Publication rights for this English edition
arranged through Kodansha Ltd., Tokyo.

Published by Vertical, an imprint of
Kodansha USA Publishing LLC, 2020

ISBN 978-1-949980-51-6

Manufactured in the United States of America

First Edition

Kodansha USA Publishing LLC
451 Park Avenue South, 7th Floor
New York, NY 10016
www.readvertical.com

Pretty Boy Detective Club

The Dark Star that Shines for You Alone

MICHIRU
FUKUROI

SOSAKU
YUBIWA

PRETTY BOY
DETECTIVE CLUB

HYOTA
ASHIKAGA

NAGAHIRO
SAKIGUCHI

MANABU
SOTOIN

Illustration Kinako, Cover Design Veia

Rules of the Pretty Boy Detective Club

1. Be pretty.
2. Be a boy.
3. Be a detective.

0. Foreword

"I disapprove of what you say, but I will defend to the death your right to say it"—so said the French philosopher Voltaire, and fitting words they are for that giant of history, since when you think about it, such a flawless method for crushing another person's opinion is hard to come by.

He first makes clear his opposition to the idea, then announces that he has absolutely no intention of debating it or even taking a seat at the table; this is exactly what is meant by the phrase "to neither kill a person nor let them live." It reminds me of the star student in class who prevents you from apologizing by claiming not to be mad in the first place.

My opinion, too, was crushed in such a way.

No, not my opinion—perhaps I should call it my dream.

This is the story of how I, Mayumi Dojima, gave up that dream. It happens all the time: A girl reaches the second year of middle school and, without a backward glance, abandons the dream she has faintly yet stubbornly clung to since childhood of "what she'll be when she grows up." So you may not want to hear such a shoddy story, but if that boy—that pretty boy—were here, I'm certain he would say this:

"Following one's dreams is beautiful. But giving up one's dreams is just as beautiful."

That's only true if you give up the dream voluntarily, however.

That beautiful boy sounds good, but that's about as far as it goes.

And in the end—what about me?

Did I say the last rites for my childish dream myself, or was it simply crushed by the surrounding pressures?

Something to think about as we forge ahead.

Finally, arrogant as this may be for someone as young and inexperienced as myself, I would also like to add one caveat to Voltaire's perfect maxim:

You can't defend anything if you're dead.

1. The Pretty Boy Detective Club

I knew vaguely that an organization going by the questionable name of the Pretty Boy Detective Club operated behind the scenes at Yubiwa Academy Middle School, the private school I attend, but fortunately I'd always managed to go about my life at school without encountering those shady characters.

Although this unofficial, undercover, uncommercial organization was reputed to resolve all types of problems at the school, its members were also rumored to be the primary cause of said problems, and so, in reality, they were viewed as a nuisance by the entire student body (aside from a small group of supporters).

While stories such as the Case of the Giant Hornet and the Case of the Multiplying Classrooms were reported as fact, however, the truth about the club itself remained a complete mystery. Even the identity of its members was uncertain, let alone its specific activities.

Everyone said whatever they wanted about it, but it

was all like an urban legend that someone had heard from a friend of a friend, and when you actually tried to talk to students who had interacted directly with the club, they kept their mouths shut. Even their all-important clients, who must have met with the members in person, refused to talk.

They'd say they were sworn to secrecy by confidentiality clauses—things like that.

Boy oh boy oh boy.

I could hardly keep from laughing. What kind of eccentric, extraordinary, or just plain execrable detectives swear their clients to secrecy instead of the other way around? They were just too enigmatic. Of course, you could say that ultimately it served to increase their mysterious aura, but when my luck unfortunately did run out and I became unwillingly entangled with them, I finally understood why their clients kept silent.

It's all so absurd that no one wants to talk about it.

After all, who likes to be called a liar for telling an unbelievable make-believe story? But I've decided to talk, even if it means being called a pathological liar.

It's not that I want to clear up the unjust and cruel misconceptions surrounding the club—nothing so admirable as that. To the contrary, I want everyone to know that those slanderous rumors don't go anywhere near far enough, which is why I'm planning to tell this story in the spirit of a whistleblower. In my case, I'm no longer bound by the confidentiality clause, so I can speak publicly.

About the Pretty Boy Detective Club.

And about those five silly-but-beautiful, and also just plain beautiful, pretty boys.

2. Four Men and One More

I was taken to the art room.

That standard art classroom that all middle schools have.

But at Yubiwa Middle School, electives have long since been removed from the curriculum, so these days the art room—like the music room, the industrial arts room, and the home ec room—sits unused.

Even though I'd been earnestly studying at this school for more than a year, I'd never been to that room.

And so I didn't know.

That a group of students had taken advantage of the fact that the room was unused to use it themselves, without permission, after school.

No—it's a bit of an understatement to say they were using it "without permission." I should probably say that they had commandeered it.

That's really the only possible word to use once you've set foot in that recklessly redecorated room.

The floors, which must originally have been unfinished wood, were covered in luxurious rugs whose pile was so deep that I couldn't help but want to kick off my shoes and bury my bare feet in them, while the fluorescent lights that must have hung from the ceiling had been replaced by not one but two chandeliers.

The standard-issue desks and bland chairs had all been removed, and in their place stood an elegant, heavy, almost certainly imported table and a couple of sofas that looked so plush I was sure my whole body would sink in if I sat down. The design of the intricately embroidered tablecloth looked exactly like a wedding veil.

The flowers in the enormous vase were arranged so naturally I could hardly imagine a human hand had placed them there, yet with an art that only a human could have achieved, brightening the whole room.

The walls covered in fresh wallpaper were crowded with paintings so famous even I recognized them, despite not being very bright about that kind of thing since I've never taken art; and in the four corners, statues that were definitely *not* plaster copies meant for sketching exercises watched over the classroom like guardian gods.

The huge cupboard in the back was lined with an eclectic collection of antique-looking ceramic and silver dishes, but rather than appearing overdone, the display was perfectly harmonious.

The built-in shelf next to the blackboard was stacked

with rare books you'd never find in the library—the kind of treasures that even an old book shop would lock away in a glass case.

Not even the clock was the same as the ones in other classrooms, but was instead a large grandfather clock that I half suspected was the one that famous song was written about.

Unbelievably, there was even a canopied bed in the room, and I could tell at a glance that it, too, was a storied antique. I didn't think I'd sleep very soundly in it, but it was made up as impeccably as the beds in the sort of luxury hotels you see in movies.

Forget art room, it was an art museum.

That was the unavoidable impression.

I froze, dumbfounded to discover that this space, so strange that it seemed almost outside the human realm, had been right there in my own middle school this whole time.

Or maybe it wasn't so much the room that made me freeze as the fact that the four boys who were lounging around in it—without a trace of guilt or shame at having broken the rules and redecorated a school facility in this way, and who, far from acting uncomfortable in their showy, show-offy surroundings, actually appeared to be in their element—were all looking me up and down.

Four boys.

The truth is, they fit into that art room perfectly—my

guess is they'd never in their lives felt the kind of visceral awkwardness I was experiencing at that very moment.

I'd been standing there motionless for a while when one of them spoke up.

"Well, well, whadda we have here? Looks like this time you dragged in a girl who's as gloomy as India ink."

Those were the words, too jeering to call a greeting, that the unfriendly-looking boy standing in front of one of the statues directed at me. This guy was seriously using a metaphor to describe my gloominess?

"She's so gloomy I bet she searches news sites for the word 'regret' just to see how many people around the world are feeling sad and then laughs about it."

Okay, that metaphor was way too specific.

Who even does that?

Those were the thoughts running through my mind, but I couldn't get them out of my mouth. I'm not the only one without the guts to contradict him—I bet you could count the number of kids at this school who would dare to do it on one hand. There might not even be a single teacher who would.

He didn't seem to know who I was, but I knew who he was—Michiru Fukuroi, year 2, class A. A legendary delinquent with a name infamous even beyond our school, and a slender build that didn't suffer one bit from comparison to the statue he was standing next to.

They called him "the bossman."

It's an old-fashioned title, but it suited his dangerous aura oddly well. One glare from the long, narrow eyes set in that fierce face of his could make a person turn and flee.

There were girls who actually burst into terrified tears at the mere mention of his name.

On the list of kids at Yubiwa Middle who you absolutely should not get involved with, he was far and away number one—and while I never expected to cross paths with him under such circumstances, now that I had, my impression was just as bad as the rumors suggested.

The funny thing—the thing that made me hesitate to write him off completely as a bad guy—was that in contrast to his ordinary appearance in the hallways of our school, here in the art room he was wearing an apron over his disheveled uniform, and a triangular handkerchief around his head.

Even as he smirked and made these nasty comments to me, he held a rag in his hand—maybe the reason he was standing near the statue was that he was polishing it?

Given that frightening face of his, the apron and handkerchief couldn't have seemed more out of place, but the mood in the room was such that I didn't feel like I could laugh or tease him about it.

However, not everyone felt the same way.

"Come now, come now, Michiru. That's no way to talk to a young lady you're meeting for the first time. I must say, you're making *me* feel quite regretful. Look, now you've gone and made the world that much sadder."

Drawn by the exquisite softness of the oh-so-refined voice chiding the infamous delinquent, I turned in its direction. And let out a mental gasp.

I hadn't recognized him before because, unlike when he was up on the stage giving speeches, his long hair was tied back in a ponytail, but now that I realized who he was, there was no question about it—no student at Yubiwa Academy could mistake the owner of that pleasant voice.

The boy gracefully sipping a cup of black tea on the sofa was the student council president himself, Nagahiro Sakiguchi. Moreover, he was no ordinary student council president—he'd held the position three years in a row. He was such a master speaker, he'd won the position the moment he delivered the address as representative of the incoming class, before the election even happened.

Among the girls at least, there wasn't a single person who wouldn't recognize that appealing voice, which captured the hearts of listeners with the skill of a voice actor.

But what was he doing here?

I couldn't contain my shock at seeing "the bossman" Michiru Fukuroi, problem child extraordinaire, in the same room as councilman Nagahiro Sakiguchi, spokesman for the honor students. On top of that, Sakiguchi had called him by his first name, like they were old friends or something…

In political terms, the top dog of the official world

and the top dog of the underworld should've been such an explosive pair that they wouldn't even have enough common ground for a conversation ... And yet this is how Fukuroi responded to Sakiguchi's reprimand:

"Oh, so you're gonna sit there and bitch to me while you're drinking the tea I made you?" He shrugged, and that was that.

The mood wasn't even faintly explosive.

And *he* made the tea? The bossman?

"Ha ha. Enough about that. The tea you made is scrumptious, Michiru."

"Hmph. Your obvious comments disappoint me, Nagahiro. I'm as disappointed as if you'd said, 'This decision is not legally binding.'"

Leaving aside the fact that Fukuroi's comment was surprisingly satirical, what was I supposed to think of this idyllic exchange between officialdom and the underworld? As I stood there dumbfounded, another voice called out to Fukuroi.

"He's right, Michi! She's an adorable girl. What are you doing telling a cute little thing like her that she looks gloomy? I almost went and proposed to her the second she walked in, like, *Hey, wanna come live with me?* Take a good look. That's not India ink, that's a Moronobu Hishikawa print. Right, cutie?"

This little speech was even more casual than Sakiguchi's.

Actually, frivolous would be a better word for it.

Leaving aside the fact that he called the universally-feared Fukuroi "Michi," where did he get off calling a gloomy character like me a "cute little thing"?

He sounded like he was taking my side, but at the same time I felt like I'd just been smoothly compared to an X-rated woodblock print, and anyway, I was hardly happy about being asked, "Right, cutie?" all buddy-buddy by this guy who was sprawled carelessly on top of the table.

Why not, you ask? Because the guy in question was Hyota Ashikaga from year 1, class A.

I don't think there's a girl in this school, or make that this city, or maybe even this prefecture, who's "cuter" than him. His perfectly proportioned face isn't just the face of an angel, it's the face of the archangel who bosses around all the other angels, topped off by a full head of bouncy hair perfectly arranged in the latest style. So whatever compliment he gave me ended up sounding like a punchy bit of irony.

Or make that a kicky bit of irony.

The uniform he was wearing had been revamped even more drastically than the delinquent Fukuroi's, with the pants practically turned into short-shorts in order to generously reveal those antelope-like legs of his that had made him the ace of the track team even though he was only a first-year.

Ever since he entered school this year looking like that, every girl who saw him stopped shortening her skirt and started wearing black stockings. That's how legendary his bare legs were.

I'd made light of all those stories, figuring they were exaggerations, but now that I saw his bare legs in real life, I realized the rumors might not be entirely groundless.

Plus, I wear black stockings myself.

"You're Mayumi Dojima, right? The second-year? I'm Hyota. Nice to meetcha, Doji. Tell me your LINE ID later, 'kay?"

Mr. Bare-Legs wasn't just friendly, he was a little too familiar. For some reason he seemed to know my name, but if he also knew I was older than him, why was he so cavalier about giving me a nickname like "Doji"?

In a sense, he was even ruder than Fukuroi. I didn't know what to say. I figured maybe I should just assume that since he was such an ace runner, he got close to people in a hurry, too.

Anyway, he could ask for my LINE ID all he wanted, but I didn't even have a smartphone.

The fact is, my communication skills are so bad that it's actually accurate to say I'm as gloomy as India ink. Hardly a minute had passed since I'd stepped into the art room, but my capacity for human interaction was already at its limit: one more word would have sent me into hysterics. Fortunately, the fourth person in the art room didn't say anything about me.

Not only that, aside from a quick glance when I walked in, he hadn't even looked at me.

He was the only one doing something appropriate to the room's original purpose—running his paintbrush over a canvas on an easel set up in one corner.

His silence rescued my emotional state by a hair's breadth—but being ignored was tough in its own way.

All the more so since *he* was the one doing the ignoring.

With all due respect to the other three—and granted, I didn't know him personally—he was even more famous than the councilman, the bossman, or the angel-among-men.

Truly.

Sosaku Yubiwa, year 1, class A.

As you can probably guess from his last name, he's the heir to the Yubiwa Foundation, the parent organization of our school—or rather, the Yubiwa Foundation is almost entirely run by this brilliant middle school student. At just twelve years old, he is for all intents and purposes the chairman of the foundation.

Put simply, he's a child genius with both money and power.

The worst possible triangle of forces.

He's not just a golden child, he's the gold standard—and therefore, if he doesn't like you, you're done for.

Not just done for, destroyed.

The highest law that all students enrolled at Yubiwa Academy Middle School must obey is this: Worship the ground Sosaku Yubiwa walks on.

So when he ignored me, I became extremely worried that maybe I'd done something to offend him—although I was probably overreacting.

It wasn't unusual for him to ignore everyone other than himself. Yubiwa never looked at anyone, and he never talked to anyone either, as if the masses were invisible to him.

No words, no interest. The iceman.

But here he was, the guy who never hung out with anyone, who wasn't part of anyone's clique because he was a one-man clique of his own, hanging out in the art room—though it would have been just as strange anywhere else, for that matter—with three other people. This was just too much.

Though if he was here, and his formidable fortune was behind it, then the bizarrely excessive décor in the room suddenly made sense. Still, seeing him here with the infamous delinquent, the most outstanding student in the history of the school, and the school idol who everyone treated like a princess was enough to make me question my own sanity and wonder if I was starting to see things.

That's how cornered I felt.

Or maybe I really had fallen from the roof *that time*—

and this was all a vision flashing before my eyes in the moment before my death.

The fact alone that these four eccentric individuals belonged to the same group was enough to practically make me faint, but to discover that on top of that they comprised the famous, or rather infamous, Pretty Boy Detective Club? Though at the same time, I found it somehow easy to believe.

Yeah, it all made sense now.

This was indeed a pretty boy detective club.

A part of me had sneered to think what overly-arrogant narcissists a group would have to be to make themselves over with such an over-the-top name, but it fit these four boys so perfectly it was almost painful.

If any other group of students had called themselves that I might have been able to tease them for it, but with these four, I couldn't say a word. It wasn't just their outward appearance, either—the way they talked and acted deserved that overblown name, too.

But that actually made me more bewildered, not less.

Why would they do it?

What had motivated these four to affiliate themselves with the Pretty Boy Detective Club, rumored as it was to be the source of all problems at our school—

"Well, since the president himself brought the client here, I won't complain," Fukuroi remarked, withdrawing his previous objections and interrupting my thoughts.

"True indeed. Shall we start by hearing the motion from the president?"

"Yeah! Pre-si-dent, pre-si-dent!"

Sakiguchi and Mr. Bare-Legs followed Fukuroi's lead. The taciturn Yubiwa still didn't say anything, but he did stop moving his brush, and this time swiveled his entire body in our direction.

"Ah ha ha ha!"

While I stood there in a daze, the person in question, the one who had brought me to the art room, laughed loudly under their respectful gazes, so different from the ones they had turned on me a few moments earlier. Then he grabbed my hand willy-nilly—and shook it as ardently as if he were hugging me.

"Once again, allow me to say how pleased I am to meet you, my dear Mayumi Dojima! I am none other than the beautiful president of the Pretty Boy Detective Club, Manabu Sotoin!"

So proclaimed the headman who commanded the bossman, the councilman, the chairman, and the angel-among-men.

Until that day, I'd never heard his name nor even laid eyes on him.

He was a pretty boy about whom I knew nothing at all.

3. Spot the Mistakes

At night, I like to look at stars from the roof of the school.

There are two mistakes in that sentence. Can you spot them?

One is a very simple, elementary error in tense—instead of "I like," I should have written "I liked."

That would be the case starting the next day.

On October 10th, my fourteenth birthday, I would stop looking up at the night sky forever.

So this was the last night.

The other mistake is a little trickier—or rather, it's one that only I could find. Because only I know about it.

But, what to make of that?

If only I know about it, maybe it's less a mistake and more a case of me being mistaken.

I'd been making the same mistake for almost ten years.

I erred with confidence and failed with pride.

But that ridiculous little tale was about to end.

I will stop my childish games when I reach my second year of middle school.

That was the promise I made to my "dear parents." I managed to interpret the words broadly, as in "until I turn fourteen," and I stuck to my old ways even after entering my second year of middle school, but the struggle seems to have been in vain.

Pointless effort. What could be more depressing.

It's better to regret doing something than to regret not doing it—the author of that famous saying is unknown, but my guess is that whoever came up with those striking words must have written them after an all-nighter or something, because the phrase is missing a crucial perspective.

It's not very common for people to regret not doing something.

No—people feel a sense of accomplishment precisely when they don't do anything.

People who say, "I should have done that!" even strike me as somehow joyful. After all, the feeling that you might have been able to do something if only you'd tried is less a regret than an aspiration.

The ones with regrets are always those who did something—so please don't tell me it's "good" that I apparently threw away ten years of my precious childhood.

Generally speaking, regret is definitely "bad."

I never imagined my life would be pointless.

What unbelievable idiocy.

Incidentally, time spent doing one thing is time not spent doing something else—and in that sense, regret over having done something may be synonymous with regret over not having been able to do anything.

If I hadn't been chasing dreams these past ten years, what might I have accomplished?

When I think about that—it's like complete devastation.

Though, when it comes to it, I can't come up with anything a person like me would have been able to accomplish anyway.

Still, I never know when to quit, so that night too I climbed up to the school roof to see what I could see, clinging to the slenderest of hopes, but nothing dramatic happened. They say that he who laughs last, laughs best. If that's true, then I suppose she who cries last also cries best.

If only I were the charming type of girl who could cry in a situation like that. I leaned on the fence around the edge of the roof and sighed, thinking despondently about the fact that in the end I hadn't managed to become that kind of girl, or for that matter, to be much of a young lady at all, and here I was about to become an adult.

"Looking for something?"

"Ack!"

The voice came from behind me at the precise moment I slouched against the fence, and my back went ramrod straight as I screamed. Since I tried to wrench myself around and look behind me while in that clumsy, in-between posture, my legs got tangled around each other and I tottered dangerously.

Oh.

Crap.

Since the roof is off-limits to begin with, the fence isn't very high. I felt my weight teetering on the fulcrum of that fence. My feet were no longer touching the ground. I had a floating sensation like I was riding an elevator—was I going to fall?

Which way? Onto this side? Or that side?

No way—was this going to be my last night in *that* sense of the word? Wait, wait, wait, you've got to be joking. How uncool would it be if everyone thought I'd killed myself at this young age because my dream had been shattered?

As I rocked back, I came to be facing straight upwards and the star-filled sky came into view—ironically, the heavens were clear and cloudless, which, as my last vista ever, wasn't too shabby.

Beautiful.

And yet.

It still wasn't the starry sky I was hoping for—

"Argh!"

I'd been lost in sentimental emotions for only an instant when a pair of arms yanked me forcefully back to "this side"—and once again, I let out an undignified scream that even I could tell was less than adorable.

I wasn't screaming about the forcible rescue, but instead about the passionate embrace into which I was pulled, as if the rooftop were a ballroom or something.

It may have been unavoidable given the unusual situation, but I'm extremely lacking in experience when it comes to being held like that—I probably would have screamed even if it had been a girl holding me, but my reaction was all the more extreme because, although small, the person holding me was definitely a boy.

I was too close to say for sure, but judging by the school uniform, he seemed to be a student at my school—still, since my social circle is so small, I had no idea who he was, what grade he was in, or if he was the same age as me, or older, or younger. He could have been an old-looking first-year or a young-looking third-year, but even if we were the same age, I was having a very hard time imagining he was a second-year student like me.

He did not look "like me." Not at all.

"Are you okay? You ought to be more careful. There's a reason the roof is off-limits, you know—it's dangerous."

As this mysterious character delivered his teacherly reprimand, his face inches from my own, I suddenly got hot under the collar—despite being the gloomy type, I have something of a short fuse. I wanted to point out that he was up here, too, and the reason I almost fell in the first place was because he started talking to me out of the blue, but the words jammed up in my throat, and instead of saying all that I stood there silently.

However, the unshakable truth was that he'd saved me from danger.

"T-Th-Tha-Thank you," I stammered—while getting my hands on his chest and pushing him away, since he was still embracing me.

"Mm-hmm."

He let go with surprising readiness—leaving me feeling quite guilty for treating my savior like a pervert. He didn't seem the least bit bothered, however.

"So you like stargazing?" he asked, looking straight up at the sky.

"Um… What makes you think that?" I asked in return, trying to gauge the proper distance between us— the physical distance, of course, but also the psychological distance, which was hard to figure out since I knew nothing about him.

"The deduction was very simple—elementary, really. That is, I can't think of any other reason why someone would be on the roof alone at this time of night."

He grinned.

His ridiculously roundabout way of talking, the haughty word "deduction," and his snarky smile didn't suit his read of the situation—at night, I like to look at stars from the roof of the school.

It would probably be absurd to tell him he should find the two mistakes in that sentence...

He started talking again, breaking into my thoughts. "I know how you feel, getting lost in those beautiful sparkling stars. I love them, too," he mused, barking further up the wrong tree. "After all, those beautiful sparkling stars do me the favor of casting me in a beautiful light."

On and on with his completely off-base—huh?

Wasn't there something odd about what he'd just said?

I did a doubletake, thinking, *Oh my goodness, I must have been so exasperated I wasn't paying attention and misheard him*, but the mysterious character just went on talking.

"Looking for something?" he asked again. "If that's the case, I'm ready and willing to help."

Help? Hardly. The whole reason I was on the verge of throwing myself off the roof in despair of the world was that he had asked me that question out of the blue.

"...What makes you think that?"

Once again, I answered his question with a question.

It was ridiculous, what did I expect from this boy I'd never even met before? There's not a person in the world who could find the mistakes in my sentence, which is to say, find my mistakes.

"Another elementary deduction. The most elementary of elementary logic. Only someone who was completely absorbed in searching for something could have failed to notice my beautiful self standing so close by."

He said that. He genuinely said that. "My beautiful self."

Realizing with terror that even if he wasn't a pervert he was definitely a sketchy character, and worse, he was standing right next to me, I was feverishly attempting to figure out an escape route when he tilted his head to the side with an inquisitive "Hmmm?" and made a comment that obliterated all my sensible thoughts.

"Oh my, how could I have been so inobservant? I was so taken by the way your long hair looked from behind that I didn't notice until now. You have very beautiful eyes."

His words didn't just obliterate my sensible thoughts, they infuriated me. I flew into a ferocious fury.

Maybe he intended them as a compliment, or maybe they were merely a social nicety, but they were the exact words I least wanted to hear—a flowery phrase that had the power to make me angrier than a hundred insults.

I took my glasses from my pocket and put them on as quickly as I could—I had to do something, anything, because even if this guy was sketchy, he was still my savior, and I was in grave danger of screaming at him. I wanted to avoid that.

"What? Why are you trying to hide those beautiful eyes of yours? What a shame to hide something so beautiful. If it's because I'm too dazzling, I'll happily dial back my aura, but you must take those glasses off at all costs. And you needn't worry that the beauty of your eyes will be dulled by standing next to me. Beauty is not something that can be compared."

Was this guy *trying* to get punched?

Jabbing away at my weakest spot over and over like that, I could only imagine he was trying to make me mad. My anger had passed the boiling point and was now going critical, which had the reverse effect of making me smile.

With a strained grin on my face, I belatedly answered his question. "Yes, I'm looking for something. Would you be so kind as to assist me?"

It's not that the sketchball was winning me over—my insane anger was just making my words come out strange. I didn't even want his help. If anything, I wanted him to disappear.

But I also wanted to give this weirdo a hard time by putting him on the spot—by gratuitously telling him my sob story. It wasn't just because he'd brought up my eyes—I was also mad that he'd interfered with my last night of stargazing, which I'd at least hoped to spend in a quiet, peaceful state of mind. Though to be perfectly honest, I also wanted to take out my feelings about the whole miserable situation on him.

Perhaps I was trying to pull this excessively cheerful boy, this perfect stranger, into the final act of my dream, which was to end this very night—but for all his talk about logic and deductions, he didn't even notice my vile scheming.

"Of course! Leave it to me. All aboard the icebreaker, full speed ahead!" he said, puffing out his chest.

To the contrary, he seemed delighted, like my request was exactly what he wanted to hear—icebreaker, huh?

He was really bending over backwards for me.

"After all, selfless service to others is the fundament of beauty! I'll need to hear your story, so come along with me—you're really in luck, by the way. All the principal members should be there today."

"M…Members?"

For some reason, I sensed dark clouds gathering.

I thought I'd done a neat job of ensnaring him in my malicious trap, but now I got the strong sense that I was the one who'd been ensnared—had I made some terrible misstep?

"Come along with you…um…where?" I asked nervously. His response confirmed my ominous hunch.

"Why, isn't it obvious? To the headquarters of the Pretty Boy Detective Club, of course!" he proclaimed proudly.

And with that, I unfortunately became involved with the Pretty Boy Detective Club, that mysterious and much-talked-about organization with which I had fortunately avoided involvement up until that day.

4. The Nature of My Request

And so, spurred on by curiosity—or rather, by the momentum of a spur-of-the-moment decision—I arrived in the headquarters of the Pretty Boy Detective Club, which is to say, the art room. But once I found myself surrounded by those four school celebrities, I withered completely.

I have the unfortunate habit of going hot and cold a little too easily—although, the net enclosing me included one obscure, or at least unfamiliar, figure.

President?

This nobody?

For all I knew he was older than me, so I probably shouldn't have been calling him "this nobody," but I found it extremely strange that these four students—Michiru Fukuroi, Nagahiro Sakiguchi, Hyota Ashikaga, and Sosaku Yubiwa—who even I, ignorant as I am of school gossip, couldn't avoid knowing about, were presided over by an obscure character whose name didn't ring the slightest bell.

I'd heard it for the first time just now.

Manabu Sotoin.

He was leaning back arrogantly on the sofa right in front of me, legs crossed... Some nerve he had, to act so self-important around this crowd.

You'd think he (as another guy) would wither all the more in the presence of his high-performing companions... Or was I just ignorant, was this Sotoin a somebody too?

Well, for the moment, if I was to judge impartially in my current cooled-off condition, apart from his arrogant attitude—going by looks alone, in other words—I'd have to say the other four had nothing on him. Pretty Boy Detective Club was an apt name indeed, egotistical though it may have been.

Hurry up and get old and fat already.

"What's this? I sense I'm being cursed," Sotoin said, peering around him. His powers of deduction may have been extremely questionable, but his intuition seemed sharp. Not that intuition could do much to "help" me—

"Well, it's not worth worrying about. Being cursed is the fate of the beautiful. Anyhow, young Dojima, tell us the details of your case. Whatever were you searching for?"

I hesitated.

I'd been planning to put him on the spot, to get him back for being such a complete nuisance, but the situation now was totally different from what it'd been on the roof. The wave I'd been riding up there wasn't going to carry me through.

Sotoin aside, I had no grudge against the other four—well, Fukuroi had been rude to me from the moment we met, but taking out my feelings on Yubiwa in particular was a horrible idea.

I might end up getting taken out myself, and not in the good sense.

Then again, even though the five of them were surrounding me, the student council president Sakiguchi was the only one I could really say was properly paying attention to me. Sotoin was still laying back arrogantly on the sofa, like he was having a meeting with the chandelier instead of me; the terrifying Yubiwa, while physically present, was obviously only there out of obligation, and was in fact facing in the opposite direction from me, like he thought looking at the wall would be more fruitful than looking at me.

Fukuroi at least did me the favor of looking at me, but clearly out of irritation. His "us guys were having a great time and then a girl had to come and ruin it" attitude was no joke—I wanted to tell him I wasn't even there of my own choosing, and anyway, he should have outgrown that attitude along with his elementary school uniform. As for Mr. Bare-Legs, he'd at least dismounted from the table, but apparently he was incapable of sitting in a normal position, or else he just wanted to show off his alluring legs, because now he was upside down on the sofa dangling them over the back.

I felt like I was at some kind of high-pressure job interview.

"..."

To hide my nervousness, I reached for the teacup sitting on the table—at Sakiguchi's suggestion, Fukuroi had included me when he made tea for the rest of the group a few minutes earlier.

Never thought I'd see the petrifying bossman pouring tea... Though, he did do it with a practiced hand.

In any case, it would be impolite not to drink the tea I'd been served.

Sakiguchi had complimented him earlier on his tea-making skills, but I figured that was mere civility, so I shouldn't expect too much. Anyway, all black tea basically tastes the same.

Still, I decided to go along with the flattery game in hopes of putting Fukuroi in a better mood, and took a sip of the hot tea—

"Ptooey!"

It was so delicious that I spit it out the instant it entered my mouth.

That's what you do when something goes down the wrong pipe, but it hadn't even gotten that far—I'd reflexively ejected it the second it touched my tongue. I was acting like they'd tried to poison me, but even with poison I wouldn't have reacted so blatantly.

"Hey, what's the problem? Does it taste that different from the sludge you usually drink?" Fukuroi asked, calmly wiping the table with a rag.

That was quite the way to put it, but actually he was right—if this was tea, then the stuff I normally drank must be tea-colored mud.

Having a guy clean up my spit-out mess was mortifying… But after that, I was able to calm down a little. Maybe it was the detoxifying effect of black tea.

The Pretty Boy Detective Club.

I had vaguely wondered what kind of person would go to such an overtly sketchy-sounding organization for help, and now I had an answer—who would've believed that the president himself went out to recruit clients?

This was no time to be spitting out tea.

Having stumbled haplessly into their net, the urgent question now was this: How do I get myself out of this art room in one piece?

Well, generally speaking, my best option was probably to apologize humbly and then leave. The very thought outraged me, but in one day I would be a grown-up. An adult. As proof that my days as a young girl (who never really experienced girlhood to begin with) were over and I could get along in the world, I ought to at least be able to bow my head to a few guys I didn't like. That was life.

"Um, I'm sorr—"

"But look at her, lads! Don't you agree that her eyes are fabulously beautiful? Look at them, look hard enough to burn a hole right through!" Sotoin cried.

I swallowed the tail end of my apology—and as all four club members (Yubiwa included) responded to Sotoin's command, staring intently at my eyes, I reflexively looked down.

"Ha ha ha! We've embarrassed her, she's blushing. Well, such modesty has a beauty of its own."

Actually, I was turning red because I was royally pissed off, but the message clearly wasn't getting through.

Screwing up my courage, I lifted my face—with a smile so tense it was practically ripping into my cheeks, abandoning myself to the sense that I didn't care what happened anymore.

"I hate beautiful people," I exploded. "Don't think everything will go your way just because you're kind of good looking."

"Kind of good looking" was a major understatement, but anyway, that's what I declared to the five of them. Even though some of them were older than me, and one—Yubiwa—had to be handled with kid gloves even though he was younger, I went ahead and had my say.

I was holding the four of them responsible for their president's words by virtue of guilt by association, but ultimately, I was the one who would take responsibility for my actions—that is, who would suffer the consequences.

The problem is, when I lose my cool, nothing can stop me—I'm a lost cause.

I was filled with regret at having flown off the handle, but at the same time, I also felt refreshed and relieved to have said it.

Anyway, I figured my comment would have the happy result of getting me kicked out of the Pretty Boy Detective Club's HQ—that is, the art room—so it all worked out.

It also worked out in relation to the fact that my girlhood was being forcibly brought to an end—while it might in fact be my entire life that ended, by this point I felt so recklessly resigned that even that would have been fine by me.

I was fully prepared for the pretty boys, their pride injured, to respond to my verbal abuse by forcefully expelling me from the room, but their reaction was completely at odds with my commonplace expectation.

One after the other, they started giggling contagiously—even the silent, expressionless Yubiwa smiled slightly.

Half of me felt like I'd accidentally glimpsed a rare treasure, while the other half felt like I was the butt of their joke, which left me unsure how to react.

"My apologies. I didn't intend to laugh, it's just— what you said was so completely typical," the student council president said, pressing his hand to his mouth.

That apology did nothing to enlighten me about what they found so funny. Typical? I was baffled.

"It's the strangest thing," Fukuroi began. "Doesn't matter if it's a girl or a guy, everyone who comes in here says basically the same thing: that beauty is worthless."

"Totally. But they all come to see the value of beauty in the end!" Mr. Bare-Legs put in with a seemingly innocent smile, still upside down on the sofa.

As I stood there tongue-tied, Fukuroi continued firing words at me.

"You're missing the point, Dojima. Like someone who reads a hit manga and says, 'If this had come out in *Jump* it wouldn't be so popular.'"

Why did this delinquent have to pepper all his key points with satire?

"For the record, young Dojima, I'd like to request one correction. It may seem like a minor point, but, like god, beauty is in the details. I will accept your use of the word 'beautiful people' as my proud burden, but I request that you take back the phrase 'good looking'—it makes us sound like we're putting on airs, wouldn't you agree?"

I didn't understand the distinction Sotoin was making. Are "beautiful" and "good looking" different?

"Of course. The first rule of the Pretty Boy Detective Club—Be pretty."

"…"

The first rule? Did that mean there was a second, too,

maybe a third?

I was getting tired of this.

But actually, if they took things that far, it could be interesting.

Yeah, things were definitely getting interesting.

I wanted to test out their claim that even I, the girl who hated beautiful people, would accept "the value of beauty" or whatever by the time we were done.

Though you could also say I was desperate.

I'd even started to feel like it was my responsibility to teach these five boys, who really did seem to think that everything would go their way, just how tough the world could be—of course, I still needed to face that reality myself, but I'd long ago stopped being rational enough to see that.

Or maybe by this point…

I was already falling under the spell of their beauty.

"Fine then. I'll accept your help."

"Mmm. You were looking for something, correct?" Sotoin prompted, his face beaming with joy as he leaned toward me.

Why was he so happy? He most definitely did not seem like the altruistic type who got his kicks by helping other people.

"A lost item, huh? What, can't find your purse or your student ID? Or maybe your dear little kitty or doggy ran away?" Fukuroi scoffed.

I felt like he was warning me that pretty boys didn't apply their powers to petty requests. He needn't have worried.

"I'm looking for a star," I said.

I'd been looking for it for ten years.

5. The Second Mistake

At night, I like to look at stars from the roof of the school.

Getting back to the second mistake in that sentence…

It shouldn't be "I like to look at stars," it should be "I like to look *for* stars"—because all this time, I've been looking for a star.

A certain star—the star I saw ten years ago.

It's impossible to imagine doing something like this today, but about ten years ago, when I was three or four, my parents, my older brother, and I went on a family vacation—we went camping for three days and two nights over a long weekend.

We swam in the ocean, cooked out on the beach, and set off fireworks.

A picture-perfect jolly itinerary.

So perfect we should have painted a picture.

But the thing that struck me most was the starry sky I saw right in the middle of our trip—I'd never seen anything so beautiful before, and I never have since.

Part of it, I'm sure, was how fresh all those sparkling stars seemed to a city kid like me.

And among them, the most beautiful one of all.

That brilliantly shining star enchanted me.

Perhaps it was the first star of evening?

It was incredibly beautiful, and seemed so close I felt like I could reach out and touch it. I didn't just want to look up at it, I wanted to visit it someday—I wanted to touch it with my own hand, and so, from that day on, I dreamed of becoming an astronaut.

I thought my parents supported that dream—but in reality, they were simply ignoring my childish, simplistic nonsense.

The truth is, it was the sort of dream that children without much common sense have. "Astronaut" is right up there with baseball player and pastry chef on the list of things that kids want to be when they grow up, so I don't think my parents were unusually unsympathetic.

To the contrary, I was the one who was mistaken, for thinking with no justification whatsoever that they understood and empathized with me.

I should have put in the necessary effort to be understood, modulated my approach so as to invite their empathy—children can't choose their parents, as the saying goes, but parents can't choose their children either.

In the end, I simply wasn't able to fit their vision of a "good child"—but when it came to pursuing my dream, another pressing problem also got in the way of building a productive relationship with my parents.

It's a very strange thing, and I tend to want to blame everything on it.

The star I saw from the shore that day?

The star that moved me so deeply, and should have determined my future—I lost it. I was sure I had seen it, but no matter how relentlessly I searched the night sky after returning from that trip, I was never able to find that star again. Not even on the last night.

To my childish mind, it was as shocking as if a part of my own body had been torn away. More specifically, I felt like my eyes had been gouged out—the two eyes that I was sure had seen that star. The shock was so great it affected the development of my personality. Everyone tried to sooth me by saying things like, "Your eyes must have been playing tricks on you," or, "That star was probably never there to begin with"—but what started out as sympathy toward a silly child transformed later into reproach for a stubborn, headstrong one.

I never got beyond a certain level of intimacy with my classmates or neighborhood friends; they didn't understand my experience. I got tired of being contradicted and started hiding the truth. That led to further isolation. And so was born a child who never bared her heart or let down her walls. At some point, in hopes of finding my lost star, I began a single-minded and solitary study of astronomical observation—I was obsessed.

Now I'm able to look back at myself in elementary school and realize that I'd gone a bit strange, but no one recognizes their own strangeness in the midst of it.

That, of course, was also the root of the split with my parents.

When it came time for me to start middle school, they finally told me straight out to get my head out of the clouds and stop dreaming—to think more seriously about my future. But I had been serious all along! I felt betrayed. This was just my own capricious belief; they hadn't betrayed me or anything, of course, but by that point I had entered my rebellious phase and become thoroughly contrary. Whatever my parents said, I wanted to do the opposite.

And then came the promise.

I will stop my childish games when I reach my second year of middle school—if by that time I had not been able to find "that star or whatever it is," then I would give up my dream of becoming an astronaut. That was the promise.

From my parents' perspective, that already must have felt like a significant compromise—I think they would have preferred I abandon my childish dreams when I started middle school.

For them, it must have all been quite unexpected.

They never guessed that I, who went hot and cold so

easily, would cling so tightly to my image of "what I want to be when I grow up"—but from my perspective, it was precisely because I had one thing to fixate on that everything else began to seem unimportant. Everything started with that star.

But that way of being—that me—is about to end.

On my fourteenth birthday, my "star search" will end.

No—it never really began.

After all, a star like that could never have existed in the first place—

6. Willing Consent

"Beautiful!"

My story was abruptly cut off by this sudden shout—but apparently shouting wasn't enough, because Sotoin jumped up from the sofa and clapped his hands loudly above his head. Really, you're still acting out your happiness like that in middle school?

"The search for a beautiful lost star! A grand case like this is perfect for the Pretty Boy Detective Club, is it not?! Right, boys?"

The "boys" Sotoin was gesturing to hadn't reached quite the same heights of excitement as him, but nor did they seem at all dismissive of my story—and that was a surprise.

As I was talking, I'd cooled down once again and taken an objective look at myself, which led me to wonder if all I was doing was giving this nasty bunch fodder for a good laugh.

"Grand… Yeah, it's grand. We don't get many requests

this grand. Well, well, looks like a shitload of work just landed in our laps." Fukuroi scratched his head in seeming irritation—which made him realize he was still wearing the handkerchief and pull it off.

He seemed reluctant to get involved, and didn't seem any less annoyed by my presence, but his words could also be interpreted as a sign that he planned to take my "case."

Actually, I felt shaken by the fact that none of them reacted with the obvious response—that is, by telling me I was stupid or saying that it's impossible to search for a star. What kind of game were they playing?

"Ah ha ha. What are you so worried about, Doji?" asked Mr. Bare-Legs. "You should be happy the president agreed to take on your case—he turns down a lot of requests at this stage 'cause they're not 'beautiful,' you know."

Was that seriously a reason for refusing a case?

Though I also didn't like the way the president had wrapped up my story in a neat little package labeled "beautiful"—did he have any idea how many bitter tears I'd shed?

"Are you saying…you're going to accept this childish request of mine? You're going to help me look for a star that I'm not even sure exists?"

"Childish is good. I'd even say it's required," Sotoin replied, flashing a peace sign.

Actually, it wasn't a peace sign—it was the number

two.

"The second rule of the Pretty Boy Detective Club—Be a boy."

Be a boy—

When I'd heard the first rule, I'd brushed it off as ridiculous, but this time I felt a jolt of surprise in spite of myself. It's not that I understood the intention behind the rule—it definitely made no sense.

And yet I felt like I'd just been told something very important.

Something I was on the verge of losing.

"Totally. We'll always stay children at heart," Mr. Bare-Legs agreed with a sunny smile. "That's why I plan to wear shorts for the rest of my life. Hyota the Adonis, he of the beautiful legs—that's me."

Seriously? What kind of a nickname is that?

He does have nice legs, I'll give him that—honestly, I get embarrassed just looking at him.

"S-So is that why you're sitting upside down, to show off your legs?"

I knew we were getting off topic, and I wasn't sure if that question was taboo, but I screwed up the courage to ask anyway since I'd been wondering.

"No way. He sits like that so his eyes are at just the right level to look up the skirts of girls who sit where you're sitting right now."

"What?!"

I reflexively tugged my skirt down the second I heard Fukuroi's explanation.

Why didn't you tell me that before?!

For his part, Mr. Bare-Legs didn't try to make an excuse or even look guilty. "Lately all the girls are wearing their skirts long, so it hasn't really been working," he complained, making no attempt to sit up normally.

Um, your gorgeous legs are the whole reason all the girls are wearing their skirts long in the first place…

Just as my indescribable rage was about to flare up again, Yubiwa quietly stood up. Of course, the cool-headed child genius wasn't leaping up in a fit of uncontainable joy like Sotoin. Far from it—he just stood up and sauntered silently out of the art room.

I didn't have time to stop him, and anyway, it's not like I had the right to. Was he leaving because he was appalled by my story? And if he was, who could blame him?

"Don't worry. The young chap is just going to make arrangements," Sotoin said, finally sitting back down— but seriously, if he could get away with calling the great Yubiwa a "young chap," who was he? Plus, anyone able to communicate with the taciturn child genius couldn't be any ordinary student.

"What…arrangements?"

"Come now, young Dojima, what on earth are you saying?"

Sotoin hadn't made fun of me when he heard my

request, but now he was definitely making fun of me. Although I hate being talked down to, the flip side was that now I knew gentlemanly courtesy couldn't explain why he hadn't laughed at my story.

In which case, did he believe me?

Had he misinterpreted my words—and mistakenly sympathized with me?

But these "arrangements"... Since it was a lost star we were searching for, he couldn't be arranging a dragnet—and if he told me he was putting up posters like you'd do for a lost dog, I'd knock him flat.

"Alright then, to the roof! Prepare for action, boys."

"Gotcha."

"Yessir."

"Will do."

The delinquent, the honor student, and the idol responded in turn and swung into action—which left me scrambling after them, to keep from being the rotten egg.

The roof? We were going back to the roof?

They probably intended to start searching the sky again—but even with six of us looking, there was no way we could find in one night what I'd failed to find for ten years. To start with, it was hard to imagine this crew, this motley crew, going about things in such a straightforward way—

"Hey, Sotoin. When you said arrangements, what exactly did you mean?" I asked, refusing to let my question go.

He answered as if he was explaining the most obvious thing in the world. "When I say 'arrangements,' what could I possibly mean but the helicopter?"

7. Flight

We boarded the helicopter that had landed on the school roof with an earsplitting roar, and before I knew it I was headed for—that is to say, whisked away unwittingly to—the same beach where I had seen that fateful star ten years earlier.

Only a few short hours after the Pretty Boy Detective Club agreed to take my case, as suddenly as if the set on a stage had been changed, I found myself standing in a place completely different from Yubiwa Academy.

There I was on a sandy beach in my school shoes.

It was indeed the same beach I had stood on ten years earlier, but my impression of it now was completely different—I felt emotionless, like none of this was real.

I did understand their logic, of course.

It made so much sense that I wondered why I'd never thought of it or done it myself—if you're going to search for something, you should look in the place you saw it last.

Not on the school roof—but on this beach.

The beach where we'd spent our family vacation.

This was way beyond elementary—this was pre-school.

Maybe I had been subconsciously avoiding this place that I hardly even remembered anymore. Maybe I didn't want to open the album of memories from the days when my family got along so well.

That delicate emotion had just been forcibly, or rather, forcefully smashed apart—and while I might understand the logic, the whirlwind speed with which this crew moved from idea to action was fairly stunning.

A bunch of middle school kids, in a helicopter?

And who was that pilot, anyway?

Well, with the power of the Yubiwa Foundation behind them, they could probably charter a nuclear submarine if they wanted… But the point worth noting here wasn't so much the helicopter itself as the fact that they'd launched such a vigorous investigation without so much as a conference or exchange of words, like they had some kind of tacit understanding.

No matter how close the five of them were, they couldn't possibly be using telepathy—which meant this must be a standard pattern for them, something so ordinary it might as well be in the manual.

The Pretty Boy Detective Club. To think that an organization with this insane level of resources was operating at my school… The rumors didn't do them justice.

Even though I was proceeding with abundant caution, I'll admit that part of me didn't take this group with its ridiculous—or rather, ridiculous-seeming—name seriously, but I needed to remember that they were actually a terrifyingly dangerous organization.

That said, this had all started with my own request, and they were doing me a favor by taking me to a place I would never have been able to get to, or even decided to visit, on my own.

Even an extreme contrarian like me knew I had to thank them.

"Th-Thank you, Yubiwa. You must be really rich…"

This time I didn't stutter as much as before, and even though I hadn't confirmed it, I was fairly sure that the funds for this little jaunt must be coming from the purse of the Yubiwa Foundation's distinguished heir—in reality, its chairman—so I directed my gratitude to Sosaku Yubiwa, but he barely twitched his lips in response.

What did he just say?

I doubt it was "you're very welcome"… Had I offended him? I suppose telling a rich boy that he must be really rich wasn't the best idea.

My reaction was too straightforward. Typical.

If only my personality could be that straightforward…

"Ha ha ha. Sosaku said he's just lucky," Sotoin explained, walking up to me.

He must take big steps for someone so short, because he was at my side in an instant.

"Sosaku is an extremely modest fellow. He always insists that he just happened to be born into a wealthy family. Don't you think that's a beautiful attitude?"

"Um…"

Given his contributions to the Yubiwa Foundation, I'd say that went a little beyond modesty… At that point, it wasn't so much beautiful as baffling and a little creepy. Still, whether leadership skills or genuine telepathy were to thank, Sotoin did appear to communicate well with Yubiwa—that is, if he wasn't making it all up.

"Of course, I'm even luckier to have met a person like him. Good fortune is a beautiful miracle. Now then, young Dojima," Sotoin pronounced, proudly and without the slightest trace of modesty, as he pointed straight above his head. "Whereabouts was your missing star?"

"Oh, um… You want to know where…?"

This abrupt plunge into the heart of the matter made me nervous.

It all happened ten years ago, so the truth was, I couldn't say anything very specific—in the process of searching for the star, my old memories must have been completely overwritten with new ones. It wasn't like they were all going to come flooding back just because I was here at the site of the original incident.

I felt like a filter had been laid over my mind's eye.

I couldn't remember.

"Do you know which constellations it was in between, where in the heavenly grid it lay? Or maybe the exact time you witnessed it?" Sakiguchi interjected.

My tension dissolved a little at the sound of that soft voice, so adept at grabbing the heart of the listener and not letting go (even the heart of an obstinate girl like me), but I wasn't able to answer either of his questions.

I began to feel embarrassed.

Had I really spent ten years searching the skies with so few clues about where to look? I might as well have been sailing the seas without a nautical chart that entire time.

I did think I'd seen it right around the same time of year, since we'd taken the trip to celebrate my birthday…

"Hmm, I see. That is indeed fortunate, since the constellations visible in summer are so different from those one can see in winter," Sakiguchi observed.

"Ha ha ha! If we find this new star that young Dojima is searching for, then there will be one more constellation in the sky! What a beautifully thrilling idea! If you insist, I will allow you to name it Sotoin after me."

The president seemed to be truly enjoying this vision of the future that he had taken the liberty of imagining… But, what? One more constellation? The part about naming it after himself was bad enough, or rather, it was terrible, but a constellation?

"Sotoin, do you maybe think that every star belongs to one constellation or another?"

"Don't they?"

Of course they don't!

There's no way all the stars in the sky could fit into the eighty-eight constellations that you can see around the world!

Well, we all have our blind spots... But he had to know about the Milky Way, at least. How many thousands of constellations would there have to be to include all those stars?

When I thought about the fact that my future depended on this ignorant bunch, I started to feel a little dizzy—their scale of operations may have been grand, but were these boys just plain old idiots after all? *Pretty* boys, sure, but an idiot is still an idiot.

"Oho, is that so?"

Sotoin wasn't the least bit shaken by my explanation.

"Unfortunately, you see, my mind is untrained—but my eye is not," he said.

"Y-Your eye?"

"That's right. I am Manabu the Aesthete, lover of beauty."

Manabu the Aesthete...

And Ashikaga had called himself Hyota the Adonis.

Don't tell me all of them have nicknames like that.

I glanced at Sakiguchi—and apparently that was

enough for him to guess my thoughts, because he declared, "While we're at it, I am Nagahiro the Orator, he of the beautiful voice." In his lovely voice.

"I can't stand the thought that you might mistake us for a bunch of boys who are only beautiful to look at. The essence of our beauty is on the inside," Sotoin announced proudly—but I was the one who couldn't stand it. I mean, he was implicitly emphasizing their physical beauty by saying that.

And, leaving aside a sense of aesthetics and a beautiful voice, weren't beautiful legs all about appearance?

Speaking of which, I'd lost sight of Mr. Bare-Legs as soon as we got off the helicopter, and when I looked around for him, I saw that he was frolicking in the surf, not only bare-legged but barefoot.

That kid has no limits.

"Ah, Hyota, always a child at heart. The paragon of the Pretty Boy Detective Club," Sotoin nodded with satisfaction. But to me, it just looked like the members of the club had forgotten their job and were playing around.

"So since you guys are pretty and you're boys, that makes you the Pretty Boy Detective Club?" I asked sarcastically.

"Oh no, of course that would never do," Sotoin replied, grinning and wagging his finger. "The third rule of the Pretty Boy Detective Club—Be a detective. You may not remember much, young Dojima, but surely you remember whether you were facing the sea or the mountains when you saw the star?"

"Oh, yeah… That much I do remember."

I was facing the sea—I think.

I hate to lump myself together with Mr. Bare-Legs, but like him, I was playing at the water's edge when I saw it—I was more focused on the ocean than the stars.

Which means that, while I can't say for certain, there's a very good chance I was facing the horizon that day ten years ago.

"Excellent, excellent. Then we'll begin our search there. Time to set up the telescope. I'll help you, Naga-hiro!"

"Understood… So I'm to be taking the lead on this, then?" Sakiguchi asked, following after Sotoin as he strode off energetically—and leaving me behind.

I noticed then that Yubiwa was gone, too.

As I was peering around in search of him, someone called out to me gruffly.

"Hey, kid. Help me get this ready."

It was Fukuroi, carrying an armload of heavy-looking bits of equipment of various sizes. They—didn't seem to be telescope parts. Which reminded me, I'd seen him busily loading up the helicopter before we left school…

"Don't call me 'kid.' Get what ready?"

"Are you stupid, kid? If I say I'm getting ready, I obviously mean the barbecue."

Obviously, huh?

When they say "arrangements" it means a helicopter, and when they say "getting ready" it means a barbecue… It's like we come from completely different cultures.

Though I doubt they'd be capable of a normal conversation, even if it were someone else they were talking to.

"What the hell are you talking about? You brought it up. You said you had a cookout with your family when you were here ten years ago."

"Oh…"

Did I say that? We swam, we cooked out, we set off fireworks.

I guess I did say that, but were they seriously planning to recreate our whole camping trip? Then, did that mean that Mr. Bare-Legs, splashing around in the waves like he was making a music video or something, was actually recreating the "swimming" part?

If that was the case, then he too was obeying the third rule of the club—and in fact, the sight of him had sparked my memory of which direction I was facing when I saw the star.

Hmm.

It seemed those beautiful legs weren't entirely useless after all—with that haughty, Sotoin-esque thought, I silently started helping get the barbecue ready.

"Well, well, I thought you'd complain more. Look at

the obedient little helper."

"…"

"Shit. You were acting all flustered and flurried until a minute ago, and now you're suddenly cool as a cucumber. What are you, a character in JoJo's Bizarre Adventure or something?"

Don't use your splendid metaphors to describe me, boy.

When he's not being satirical, he's just plain good.

"My parents always said that those who don't work don't eat. Trained me well," I answered.

"Trained you, huh? Sounds like your parents were pretty strict. And like you don't respect them much."

As Fukuroi talked, he was getting everything ready so efficiently he hardly needed my help. But while it was a keen observation, I felt like he was twisting my words, which didn't sit well with me.

"Guess things would've been easier if I was a rebel like you."

Which is why my response was so nasty.

My own lousy personality was driving me crazy. On reflection, I was also being fairly reckless—why on earth would I want to antagonize the bossman, whose name was notorious well beyond our own school?

Maybe I'd been numbed by the fact that we were setting up for a barbecue together by the beach, but under normal circumstances this was not a guy that someone like me would even have the guts to talk to.

"Good point. No way I could've spent ten years searching for a star that might not even exist."

I'd been secretly quaking in fear that he was going to grab me by the collar or something, but his response was surprisingly mellow. Without another word, he pulled some meat and vegetable chunks that he must have cut up in advance out of the cooler and started putting them on skewers.

He sure was good at all of this... He still had his apron on from when we were at school, and at some point he'd put the handkerchief back on his head, so all in all, he reminded me more of a lunchroom worker than a juvenile delinquent. Although the handkerchief didn't fully hide that fierce face of his (actually, it made him look even scarier).

I wasn't trying to be competitive, but after I finished setting up the grill, I made a move to start helping him skewer the vegetables and meat—however...

"Idiot, what are you doing?! Stop skewering the meat so carelessly! Each piece has to be skewered the right way!"

...He was furious.

He hadn't blinked an eye at my snide remark, but now that I was skewering the meat on the wrong side, he couldn't contain himself?

"Just stop. Go and set the table! And don't lay another

finger on the food!"

Some nerve, considering he's the one who told me to help in the first place… Girls are supposed to like guys who can cook, but if Fukuroi was going to act this tyrannical, I'd have to call him an exception to the rule.

It would be bad enough if he were cooking fancy Italian pasta or something, but throwing his weight around over typical guy food like barbecue?

Anyway, I'm fairly sure that when my family cooked out ten years ago, we didn't pay much attention to how the meat was skewered—which meant the reenactment was going to outdo the original?

"I doubt it makes a difference how you skewer the meat."

"Did you say something?!"

Nope, not me.

Keeping my distance from the lunchroom-cook-slash-exacting-craftsman, I bravely and briskly got started on my assigned task of setting the table. "Setting the table" was a bit of an overstatement anyway, when all I had to do was lay out some paper plates and cups—or so I thought, until I realized that the silver dishes from the art room had been loaded onto the helicopter.

Was this their everyday tableware?!

Even the cups were porcelain, and the chopsticks were spellbindingly beautiful lacquerware—none of it matched, and there was a bewildering mix of Western and Japanese styles, but it was all very fancy even if it had nothing else in common.

Which reminds me, I was too nervous earlier to pay close attention, but the tea I drank in the art room had been served in a peculiarly extravagant teacup as well...

"Sh-Should we really be using this stuff? Seems like kind of a waste..."

"What are you talking about? They're dishes, it would be a waste *not* to use them."

The delinquent apparently had good ears, because he picked up my mumbled comment and responded in an annoyed tone.

Though his point was well taken, I must admit.

"But aren't these historical treasures or something?" I protested vaguely, since I had no idea what I was talking about.

"No way. He made them."

"Really? Made them?"

I turned my head in the direction Fukuroi was pointing with his skewer of meat—and caught sight of the first-year child genius, who'd disappeared earlier.

Sosaku Yubiwa.

He was playing by the shore, building a sandcastle.

Actually, his expression was way too serious for the word "playing"—in contrast to his usual blank emotionlessness, his face now displayed the utmost earnestness, even though he was wielding shovel and bucket to pile up sand.

Wait, was this supposed to be another reenactment of the bygone me?

Though, I don't think I mentioned playing in the sand…

Yubiwa didn't look younger than me, but he was actually the same age as Mr. Bare-Legs, so maybe he was still a child at heart, too?

"He's good with his hands. You hadn't noticed? Most of the paintings and sculptures in the art room are copies he did."

No, I hadn't noticed.

I'd assumed the little rich boy had bought all that stuff with his bottomless expense account, and that probably was true for some of the pieces—but not all of them, apparently. Wow. The word "copies" might sound cheap, but in a sense I bet it's harder to make counterfeits that good than it is to get your hands on the originals.

I took my glasses off to get a better look at his castle, and noticed that it bore a striking resemblance to the Sagrada Familia…

Just what did that child genius imagine the childhood me had been capable of?

There was nothing the least bit childlike about that sandcastle.

"With his family business and everything, he plays a major role in the financial world, but what that guy really loves is detailed creative work. Sosaku the Artiste, creator of beauty—that's him."

"Sosaku the Artiste…"

Huh. So that art room was pure Yubiwa.

Makes sense, I thought to myself as I examined the silver plate I held in my hands. If he had the creative genius to make something like this, then I guess he really could say he "just happened to be lucky" enough to be born into that family.

Of course, he technically hadn't said anything himself.

Sotoin just said he said it. The eccentricity of the president, who made a show of commanding a genius like Yubiwa, was becoming clearer and clearer.

"Hello, Earth to Dojima. Hurry up with that. I'm done getting the skewers ready, so I'm gonna start cooking. Do you even realize how much work goes into cooking for six?"

"No, not really…"

There was so much I didn't know.

I mean, until now I hadn't even been sure the Pretty Boy Detective Club was real.

"I had no idea you and Sakiguchi were friends, either. I've never heard anyone mention anything like that."

"What? Friends? Quit messing with me. You're the kind of person who starts clapping to the beat and then doesn't know when to stop."

Yeah, his non-satirical metaphors were definitely gentler than his satirical ones, but he still sounded irritated.

"We don't talk to each other when we meet in the halls. Our ceasefire only applies in the art room—only under the supervision of the president. And that doesn't just go for Nagahiro. The president's the only one Hyota will listen to, and the only one Sosaku will talk to. If it weren't for him, we'd never manage to come together as a group. You're right about that, at least."

"..."

His words sounded somehow cold—but still, "we."

That word he used so easily made me weirdly envious.

Wouldn't it be nice.

I wish I could lump myself together with someone else like that.

Actually, my feelings went beyond envy—I was straight-up covetous of their bond.

"...Um, Fukuroi, how serious are you guys?"

"Huh? Whaddaya mean?"

He furrowed his brows like he had no idea what I was talking about.

"You guys just met me, I'm nothing to you, my story is nothing to you, but you're doing all this for me. I don't think you're motivated by a passion for community service, right? So is the Pretty Boy Detective Club just a hobby for a bunch of kids with too much time and money on their hands?"

"…"

"I mean, the helicopter and everything. I'm grateful for that, and I know I'm indebted to you, but… I feel like you think my problems are silly, and honestly, I'm not very happy about that. I feel like me and my case have been swept up by special people with excellent character design who do everything on a grand scale."

I was laying it all out very bluntly. I was talking shit.

I realized that.

But I couldn't stop the torrent of words.

"It's like this is all a game for you guys. I'm not your toy, you know."

"Ha."

I was ready for him to abandon my case on the spot and tell me to go home, but he just laughed.

"Bo-ring. You've got it all wrong. 'Excellent character design,' what kind of shit is that? We're not characters in some anime."

"Uh…"

"You're like one of those people who thinks kids these days play so many video games that they start to believe people will come back to life if they hit the reset button. I mean, adults are the ones who visit graves and have funerals and believe a bunch of illogical shit about dead people."

This time the satire was out in full force. Did he get

more satirical when he was on the attack?

At least let us have our graveyard visits.

"Eat. You're the poison taster."

He held out a skewer of meat that he'd grilled without my even noticing—I guess he'd lit the barbecue and started cooking while I was in the midst of baring my soul.

I took the skewer, wondering if he'd even been listening.

Poison taster, huh?

Maybe he was expecting a dramatic reaction on par to when I drank the tea, but come on, barbecue tastes the same whoever makes it.

"Don't eat it all dainty like that. Open your mouth and shove the whole thing in."

This guy had no subtlety.

Still, there wasn't any other way to eat that big hunk of meat, so I shoved it in.

"Ptooey!"

I spit it out. Once again, like I'd been served genuine poison. Like a genuine poison taster.

"Hey! Stop fooling around! You just wasted a good piece of meat!"

He got mad about the weirdest things. Apparently using the good silver at a barbecue wasn't a waste, but spitting out a piece of meat was. I didn't get it.

"It tastes so different from the lumps of rubber I usually eat… My stomach couldn't handle it…"

"You said it, not me."

I had that one coming, but for once, I'd given my honest opinion—it was hard to believe that the way meat was cut and grilled could affect the flavor this much.

Or rather, the texture...

It was so succulent I wanted to drink the juices and leave the rest.

"N-No way, don't tell me you're crying."

Fukuroi drew back, and I realized then that tears were pouring down my cheeks from the incredible deliciousness—oops, looks like I made the bossman uncomfortable.

"I-I'm not crying. I just got some meat juice in my eye."

"Sounds painful... Are you okay?"

"Don't worry about me... sniff sniff."

So embarrassing.

So uncool.

I mean, crying in front of a guy?

To cover it up, I put on my glasses, which had been off this whole time. Then to cover it up some more, I said sharply, "Ha, ha haah. S-So you must be Michiru the Epicure or something?"

"He of the beautiful palate, yeah. What's so funny about that? Stop talking to me like we're enemies. I'm on your side... Geez."

Fukuroi picked up the piece of meat I'd spit out and

started carefully brushing off the sand, even though it must've still been hot.

I was still debating how to take his casual statement that he was on my side, and also thinking that he didn't need to make a fuss over cleaning off the meat if he was just going to throw it away, when he blew my mind by popping it into his mouth.

Before I even finished registering shock, he was noisily chewing away.

"Ooh, that is good. No one does it like me. Hm? What's with you? Awww, are you thinking, 'Eee, a second-hand kiss!' or something?"

"No, I am not thinking anything remotely like that."

Considering he was eating something I'd spit out, the situation was a bit beyond a second-hand kiss. The only thing I was thinking about was the question of hygiene—because it had been on the ground, of course, not because it had my saliva on it.

"Nothing to worry about. I used to live on food that other people dropped on the ground—wasting good food bothers me a lot more than a few germs. That attitude evolved into Michiru the Epicure—and thanks to Sosaku, I can buy expensive ingredients now, which I'm super grateful for."

"..."

Since the child genius was so far outside the norm, I'd assumed the other members of the club must be rich, too, but I guess that wasn't the case. Still, however much Fukuroi liked metaphors, "living on food that other people dropped on the ground" sounded like a pretty rough childhood.

The part about excellent character design aside, maybe I'd been unfair to call them special people who do everything on a grand scale. The more I thought about it, the more that seemed to be the case. And the more my own shallowness started to bother me. To cover it up, I popped an onion from the skewer into my mouth, and—

"Ptooey!"

"Okay, enough already!"

With great difficulty, and wailing with each bite, I managed to finish a whole skewer.

"Hey, wipe your mouth and tears and look at that idiot," Fukuroi said, handing me his handkerchief.

Manabu Sotoin, president of the Pretty Boy Detective Club, was peering into the wrong end of the telescope with a persistence that bordered on obstinance.

Seriously, he brought along that ostentatious telescope without even knowing how to use it? Apparently the line about his mind being "untrained" wasn't just a rhetorical flourish to highlight his outstanding aesthetic sense. Sakiguchi, who was standing near him, looked equally exasperated.

"That is one serious idiot," Fukuroi observed.

" ... "

Leaving aside the fact that he was calling his own leader an idiot—and also the fact that that selfsame leader evidently didn't know how to use a telescope—the sight of Sotoin amusing himself by searching for stars as excitedly as Mr. Bare-Legs was playing in the surf really was a far cry from anything you could call "intellectual."

A far cry, but...

"As you can see, he's already forgotten that all of this started with you. Even if you asked him to drop the case right now, I doubt he'd stop looking for that lost star. That's his brand of seriousness—and his aesthetic."

"..."

"If our leader is serious about something, then we're serious about it. Don't worry. No one thinks your problems are silly, and no one is looking down on your dreams. In fact—"

Fukuroi paused for a second.

"I think the person who looks down on your dreams the most might be you."

8. The Client's Thoughts and Opinions

A reenactment of a family camping trip.

As I thought about that, a faint chill ran through me.

What was I getting all nostalgic about?

Or, getting delusional about, more like. After all, there's no way my family will ever take a vacation together again.

That wasn't going to change, even if I gave up my dreamlike dream of becoming an astronaut and turned into a grown-up—even if I improved my attitude, I could never go back.

The cracks would never be filled in.

What's lost is lost for good.

Maybe that's what not only this camping trip but the whole past ten years were about—maybe I wasn't chasing after something that might or might not exist, but instead something that *couldn't* exist.

Because as long as I was searching for it, I could hold onto my dream.

How idiotic.

If I wanted to become an astronaut, why didn't I just focus on studying? I should have been practicing those all-white jigsaw puzzles they say are part of the astronaut exam. Anyway, communication skills are supposed to be even more important for astronauts than language skills—if it's so crucial to get along with everyone, did I think I was going to succeed with this hopelessly difficult, warped personality I'd developed?

While I was chasing my dream.

I had become a petty, ill-natured, jealous, servile person—which is the saddest thing that can happen to anyone.

I know my personality is lousy, but there's no way to fix it—and if having to live with that person for the rest of my life isn't hell, then I don't know what is.

Sotoin said my dream was beautiful.

He praised the beautiful idea of rediscovering a lost star. By the time we got to the beach, I couldn't really question the sincerity of his words—but I still rejected them.

I didn't want him dressing up my suffering with a nice word like "beautiful"—and I was furious that he would use my troubles and dreams as a way to pass the time.

But those weren't my real feelings.

I didn't just look down on my dreams.

I was repulsed by them.

At some point, the dreams we chase after become hideous.

So maybe I hadn't spent the past ten years chasing my dream after all—maybe I'd been running from it.

9. With the Dawn

Not to give away the ending, but even though the Pretty Boy Detectives and I searched the sky until it began to grow light, we achieved nothing.

Well, when you get right down to it, I have to concede that the child genius's Sagrada Familia might count as an achievement, but even those lofty spires rising from the sand fell victim to the merciless bare legs of Mr. Bare-Legs.

An act of destruction carried out with a brilliant smile.

Even naivety can go too far.

Considering Yubiwa had spent the whole night building his castle, it was more the act of a demon than an angel, but the victim just shrugged. Such a big heart.

And a big wallet to match.

Anyway, we took turns napping, eating barbecue, setting off fireworks and the like, but by the end of the night, although we'd made full use of the telescope to examine not just the sky over the sea but every corner of it in every direction, all we'd found were existing celestial bodies.

"Existing celestial bodies" is a strange phrase, but in any case, what I mean to say is that we did not find the new star that I saw ten years ago—the new star that I and I alone saw ten years ago, and which I'd been stubbornly insisting I really did see ever since.

I'd be lying if I said I wasn't discouraged, but common sense told me this would probably happen—after all, how often does a person spend ten years looking for something and then dramatically discover it on the very last night?

Anyway, encountering the Pretty Boy Detective Club was drama enough. Expecting more would be asking for punishment—although from my perspective, meeting them on the last night was itself a kind of punishment.

Searching the sky from the location of the original sighting had some logic to it, but that said, we were still in Japan. Given that our school and the beach weren't in different hemispheres, the stars visible from each place wouldn't be very different, and since we weren't professional stargazers, the outcome was bound to be basically the same.

Plus, as far as accurately reenacting the past goes, I hadn't had a telescope ten years ago. And so I greeted the morning of my fourteenth birthday empty-handed.

The appointed morning.

On this day, ten years' worth of dizzying, dreamlike days would come to an end—and at long last, I would be freed from my nightmare.

Still, I felt an extra twinge of regret that the day was unfolding exactly as originally planned, only now with the addition of four school celebrities (plus one obscure figure) roped into it.

But either way, my time was up.

It was an ordinary weekday with ordinary classes, which meant we middle school students had to be heading back—though of course I'd broken my curfew hours and hours ago.

That was fine by me, but didn't any of these guys have a curfew? Unlikely, I guess. They didn't exactly seem to be bound by the rules of the ordinary world.

Anyway, since all I'd shown them so far was my less-than-charming side, I decided the time had come to apologize and thank them humbly, or if not humbly, then at least frankly, but—

"It's still too early to give up! I can reach no other conclusion!"

Sotoin's war cry demolished my frank and humble good intentions. And then resentment boiled up at this idiot for ruining my touching sentiment.

Forget touching, I was back to touchy.

Though apparently I wasn't the only one who didn't get his point.

"What do you mean, dear leader?"

A question arose from one of his minions.

A question asked in the dulcet tones of Nagahiro the Orator.

If someone asked me a question in that voice, I think I'd fall all over myself to be accommodating, but the leader was unfazed.

"Young Dojima's promise to her parents takes effect when she turns fourteen, correct? At what time of day were you born, young Dojima?!"

"Wh-What time?! Um, in the evening, I think…?"

Although I didn't know the exact time, I remember my grandmother saying something like that before she died—but, really?

"Yes, really. In other words, we're in overtime until evening!"

His logic rendered us all speechless.

I'd already stretched the deadline from the second year of middle school until my fourteenth birthday, but he was really splitting hairs here—seriously, wasn't overtime taking it a little too far?

He smiled smugly, as if to say, "See what I did there?"

"Okay, but…" I managed, gripping my head as I tried to figure out how to dissuade him.

Maybe he'd had so much fun stargazing that he wanted to keep going, which was a boyish motivation perfectly in line with Rule #2 of the Pretty Boy Detective Club, but still…

"Even if your logic is solid, it's no good. And by no good, I mean good-for-nothing."

"Good-for-nothing? What do you mean by that?"

Sotoin tilted his head, as though he thought the phrase "good-for-nothing" wasn't very beautiful—but I'm pretty sure my meaning was clear without a point-by-point explanation.

"It'd be one thing if we had the whole night, but we're talking evening. The sun is already rising, and by the time the stars come out again, the clock will have run out."

I could postpone the buzzer, but if it went off before nightfall, the extension was pointless—kind of like pushing back an execution by a few hours.

I'd feel better if they just chopped my head off here and now.

"You don't get it, do you, young Dojima. You can see certain celestial bodies, like the sun and the moon, during the daytime, can you not?"

"Well, sure, if you're talking about the sun and moon…"

It was no good. Not good-for-nothing, just no good.

I couldn't persuade this boy—so I looked to the student council president, who seemed to have known him the longest, for help.

I knew I could count on that beautiful voice.

Plus, someone had mentioned that Sakiguchi was

vice president of the Pretty Boy Detective Club—but he just gave me a pensive look that rivaled Sotoin's smug one.

Don't tell me Sotoin's argument had actually won him over…?

Fukuroi seemed to have the same concern. "Come on, Nagahiro. You're not actually in favor of this idiotic idea, are you?"

Apparently, he wasn't any more hesitant to call the president an idiot to his face than behind his back, which I suppose you could say was candid of him—and the president didn't seem the least bit bothered by it.

"Come now, Michiru. Just because an idiot comes up with an idea doesn't mean the idea itself is idiotic," the student council president replied, putting the bossman in his place.

And once again calling the president an idiot.

Somehow, even though he led the Pretty Boys, they didn't seem to respect him.

"What do you mean, Nagahiro? I doubt we'll be able to see any stars in the daytime," Mr. Bare-Legs asked, rubbing sunscreen onto his vaunted legs with unexpected conscientiousness as the sun began to rise.

"I have a theory—and I'd like to test it out. Ms. Dojima," Sakiguchi turned toward me. "As soon as you get home, please insist that your parents go along with our leader's proposal. Even if they don't see his logic, I'm sure they will concede to a mere half-day extension. And after school, may we request the pleasure of your company in the art room once again? I believe we may have some good news for you."

Despite the polite veneer on his words, his tone left no room for opposition—and how could I say no to that beautiful voice?

Anyway, he was the only club member with any semblance of common sense, and since I figured there wasn't any harm in doing what he said, I nodded in self-interested agreement.

Even as I shuddered in disgust at my own filthy heart.

But of course, the word "theory" piqued my interest.

A theory—what theory could hold up at this late stage of the game?

"Ah ha ha. Don't expect too much, Doji. This fellow may look respectable compared to us, but he's got a Lolita complex. His girlfriend's in first grade."

"What?!"

When I heard this momentous announcement, delivered so nonchalantly by Mr. Bare-Legs, I hugged my chest and took a single step back—and a hell of a lot more than one on the inside.

"Ha ha ha. There's nothing to be afraid of, young Dojima. If you look past the lolicon, a guy like Nagahiro is a rare find these days," Sotoin put in.

Oh no, nuh-uh.

The best eyes in the world couldn't look past something like that.

"Stop saying such disreputable things, you two… She's not my girlfriend, she's my fiancée. Our parents arranged the engagement without consulting us. The president knows that perfectly well, I believe."

Judging from Sakiguchi's calm response, this seemed to be a running gag—both the delinquent and the child genius just ignored the whole exchange. If this sort of black humor was part of their standard routine, they'd better be prepared to lose some fans…

Although the news that Sakiguchi was engaged would probably lose him plenty of fans already—mostly female ones.

I was so caught up in worrying about things that were none of my business, I completely missed Sakiguchi's next mumbled words.

"But he may be right to say that you shouldn't expect too much."

10. Reflections and Shadows

My parents were easy to convince. Or maybe I should say they were so sick of my shenanigans they didn't have the energy to object.

In any case, they extended the promised deadline to that day at sunset—and I reached a new and humiliating level of poor sportsmanship. I felt like crawling into a hole. I doubt I'll ever be able to use the word "promise" again.

I scarfed down my breakfast, rinsed off my sweat in the shower, shook off my sleepiness and headed back to school—although Yubiwa Academy is private, it's close enough for me to walk to, and I figured that if I hurried, I'd just barely make the warning bell.

I'd never call myself a star student, but on paper at least I've always been a healthy young girl with an unbroken record of zero tardies or absences. As I hurried along, the road to school abruptly yanking me back to reality after the events of the previous night, I thought things over.

It goes without saying that I was thinking about what

theory Mr. Lolicon, I mean Honor Student, might have come up with—but I had no clue.

Far from simply throwing cold water on the president's excitement, he seemed to have had something similar on his mind the whole time he was watching the stars—which reminded me of a comment he made while we were eating the barbecue.

"It's quite a mystery that while not only we but people all over the world have been observing the skies, no one has yet found your star. The discovery of a new star, let alone the disappearance of one, would surely be the talk of the astronomical community."

This further spurred the enthusiasm of their leader, who exclaimed, "We must find it before anyone else does!"

That sent the conversation off track, but I don't think that was what Sakiguchi was trying to say.

Normally, his point would lead to the disappointing conclusion that I'd been mistaken all along, but then the whole thing would end there—without connecting to any "theory."

It was no good. I couldn't figure it out.

I would just have to wait until school got out—and I'd better be sneaky about going to the art room, because if anyone found out I was hanging around those famous boys, I might lose what few friends I had...

I had mixed feelings about the weird way my girlhood

was ending, when it was supposed to have concluded so quietly—why had things turned out this way?

Why so weird, and so wearisome?

It all stemmed from my own obstinance when I first met that bizarre character on the roof of the school—in that sense, I had this coming to me. I was responsible for everything because I hadn't been able to control my own flood of emotions.

Still, when someone mentions my eyes, I can't help—

"Crap."

Now I'd done it.

I realized that I'd accidentally left my glasses on the bathroom sink, where I put them when I took my shower—and since I was already on the verge of being late for school, I unfortunately didn't have time to go back and get them.

I'd have to go to school without them… Ugh, I wish I'd never even noticed. This wasn't the first time I'd forgotten them (it happens surprisingly often), but when I thought about the fact that I would have to see that insensitive president of the Pretty Boy Detective Club after school, my already weighty mood sank below sea level.

"I'm doomed…"

I considered whether I might be able to make it home and back in time if I ran at full speed, decided it was impossible, and was just turning around anyway when I saw it.

I saw something I didn't want to see.

A figure, shadowing me.

"... ～ ♪ "

I instantly started whistling and let the momentum of my turn carry me a full three hundred and sixty degrees—it was an extremely mediocre way of covering up the fact that I'd spotted them, but I'm not such a weirdo as to seek aesthetic perfection at a time like this.

But given that I'm not a weirdo, why would an adult need to be tailing me?

Leaving aside the question of what else you could call a girl who spins around and whistles on her way to school—an adult?

I hadn't seen the figure clearly, but it was ... an adult.

Thinking it would seem strange if I stopped moving, I started walking again at the same rapid pace as before, trying to look as natural as possible—but it was no good. My right arm and right leg both went forward at the same time.

I wondered ... Had they noticed that I noticed them?

That would be bad.

I'd brushed off the need to carry a personal alarm around with me, and even if they'd been allowed at school, my parents hadn't even bought me a flip phone, let alone a smartphone.

Unfortunately, having overheard that conversation earlier in the morning about guys with a thing for underage girls, I was feeling extra nervous. I may be overly self-conscious, but I'm not overly self-confident, so while I don't tend to be conceited like the guys in the Pretty Boy Detective Club, I do realize that the mere fact of being a girl in middle school may give me value in the eyes of some people—so now what do I do?

Head for school as fast as possible.

I'll be safe on school grounds.

But I'd better not walk too fast.

Basically, since I'm not an athlete, there's no way I could beat an adult male in a footrace—oh man, say this isn't happening to me! Why do I have to deal with this crap just because I'm a girl, when I clearly don't have time for it right now?

No, calm down, calm down, this could all be a misunderstanding.

Maybe it just looked like they were following me.

Being so sleep-deprived, it was entirely possible I'd made a mistake.

The so-called normalcy bias was making me try to reconcile my wariness and sense of danger with the reality that crazy adventures don't happen very often in real life. I was planning to reassure myself when I reached the next corner by glancing casually over my shoulder, but when I got there, something else happened.

On the far side of the corner, I saw something else I didn't want to see—two adults, standing there like they were waiting for me.

Two—plus the one behind me made three.

Hey, I must be really hot!

Wouldn't it be great if I had the kind of sunny personality that could make a joke like that? But the real me was just an easily upset, easily freaked out girl with no sense of humor.

Even with someone tailing me and two other people lying in wait, I should have remained calm, pretended I didn't notice, and rushed directly to school. But I'd already lost control of myself, so instead, I reflexively turned down an alley—leading in the opposite direction from school.

And then, of all things, I took off running.

They say that if you meet a bear in the woods, the only thing worse than playing dead is running away—but this time, I'd gone and done everything you weren't supposed to do.

My brain wasn't working right.

I didn't escape to school, I didn't go home—instead, even though I had no idea what was going on, I just started running like crazy. It might not've helped, and it might've even made things worse, but every time I came to a corner, I turned.

Crap. Crap, crap, crap!

Why is this happening to me?

If they had the time to follow me and wait for me

around corners, they ought to be stalking the bare-legged idol of our school, Hyota Ashikaga!

Even at this late stage I was still hanging onto the hope that I was imagining everything due to hyper self-consciousness, but that hope was alas naïve—after turning right who knows how many times, by chance I succeeded in doing what I'd tried to do before, and looked behind me.

I succeeded, but like Orpheus carelessly disobeying the warning not to turn around as he led Eurydice back to the land of the living, I was consumed with regret.

What I saw actually was like a vision from another world.

Three followers? I wish.

Close to ten adults were running after me now—all kinds of people, and not just men anymore, but women as well.

I was beyond confused.

This was no stalker with his sights set on a middle school girl who wasn't even popular with guys her own age—more like a mob pursuing a criminal on the lam.

What the hell is going on?

"Ack!"

In any case, I still have the least charming scream ever.

Since my attention was focused behind me, I hadn't noticed what was up ahead, and as I leapt out of the alley onto a main thoroughfare after another right turn, I almost ran headlong into a bicycle—or more accurately, it came at me sidelong as if to block my way.

Had they headed me off at the pass?!

Or were even more than ten people after me? If so, this pincer attack had caught me like a rat in a trap—game over. For an instant, I was plunged into despair—but the person on the road bike wasn't an adult.

It was a kid.

He was wearing a helmet and workout gear, so the initial impression he gave was different from when we were at school, but once I noticed it, there was no mistaking that dazzling sparkle—which was emanating from the gorgeous pair of bare legs protruding from his shorts.

It was the bare-legged idol of our school, Mr. Bare-Legs himself.

As I hesitated in confusion, he reached out a hand and shouted in an uncharacteristically serious voice, "Get on!"

11. Riding Double

He told me to get on, but this was a road bike.

Before I could even get to the ethical question of the fact that riding two to a bike violates the traffic code, I had to confront the fact there was no cargo rack—so how the hell was I supposed to "get on"?

If I'd been in a calmer mood to start with, I probably would have been so flustered by the situation that I wouldn't have been able to do anything at all, but since I was panicking over the unprecedented dilemma of being chased by something like ten adults, I was far from calm.

Which is why I made up my mind so quickly.

Without hesitation, I threw myself onto Mr. Bare-Legs in a full-frontal hug—my arms and legs wrapped around him like a koala on a eucalyptus tree.

It was a perfect cheek-to-cheek embrace.

There's a limit to how much immodesty one can take, but I didn't have time to think about that—the only thing I could think about was how to escape.

Actually, I wasn't even thinking.

I didn't think about anything, I just clung to him wholeheartedly—with my whole body.

He looked delicate, and until last year he was actually in elementary school, but guys are guys, and he didn't even flinch at me hanging onto him in that weird position.

I could even detect a slightly muscular build beneath his clothes.

"Zip it!"

At first, I took that as a truncated suggestion for how to keep warm on our ride, but as soon as he started pedaling I realized he meant "don't talk"—that's how fast we were suddenly going.

The second I tried to talk, I would have bitten my tongue.

As I was imagining the kind of passionate woman who would bite her tongue and die with her arms wrapped around a boy, Mr. Bare-Legs tore away from the mob of adults, and fresh scenery surrounded us.

He was way faster on his bike than on some half-baked motorcycle.

Ohhh...

He of the beautiful legs.

Maybe it wasn't just about superficial beauty after all.

Speaking of which, he didn't come off as an athlete, but he was an ace member of the track team even before he was the school idol. Completely unhindered by the fact that he was supporting my entire weight (although actually, I was using all my own strength to cling to him), he pedaled us forward without even needing to stand up. Those legs weren't just pretty to look at—their beauty went to the core.

When the figures pursuing me had disappeared completely into the distance, I belatedly realized Mr. Bare-Legs had rescued me.

Oh crap.

I suddenly felt very ashamed to have wished that the adults would stalk him instead of me, even if it was my own little secret.

As I was reflecting on how to atone for my willfulness, my savior, to whom I was still clinging, went and opened his ridiculous mouth.

"Ah ha ha. Doji, your boobs are surprisingly big."

Don't think you can get away with saying anything you want if you use that cheerful tone, buddy.

With that, the surprisingly muscular first-year did me the favor of absolving me of my guilt.

12. Sabotage

Thus did the modest record of zero tardies and zero absences held by second-year middle school student Mayumi Dojima meet its end: I was late to school on the morning of my fourteenth birthday.

Thanks not only to the speed of his bicycle but also to his excellent knowledge of geography, Mr. Bare-Legs zigzagged through the streets after shaking off the mob of adults and, after a roundabout journey, delivered me to school. Unsurprisingly, however, the last bell had long since rung by the time we arrived.

I'd never been particularly obsessed with my record, but I still felt a pang of regret to see it end—after I entered the school building and allowed myself a sigh of relief, a vague sadness washed over me.

"Uh-oh, we're late. Well, whatever. I may as well skip all my classes today!"

On the other hand, Mr. Bare-Legs—who wasn't even breathing hard after that long ride—seemed positively delighted. Seriously? What kind of overly free spirit takes the whole day off just because he's late?

I was beginning to suspect that, though it was hard to tell since he was cuter than most girls, even, this guy was actually the most dangerous member of the Pretty Boy Detective Club.

"Well, I'm off to the art room. How about you?"

"Uh, I'm not sure…"

I may not be a star student, but I knew that if I wanted to play the good girl, I should tiptoe into class even though first period was already half over. But more than that—more than anything—I needed to ask Mr. Bare-Legs for an explanation.

I was thankful he'd rescued me. My gratitude was boundless.

But his timing was just too good.

It stretched credulity that the dashing hero just happened to appear at the moment I was being chased by that mysterious mob of adults—if dramatic adventures don't exist in real life, then that kind of rescue *definitely* doesn't.

Since it *had* happened, then obviously there must be some explanation—and I needed to know what it was.

"What's this? You want to get me alone? Dirty girl!"

By now he was well past the point of absolving my guilt and into the territory of triggering my gag reflex, but in any case, Mr. Bare-Legs and I headed off to the art room together.

To the headquarters of the Pretty Boy Detective Club.

...The events of the previous night seemed totally unreal, like a fuzzy dream, but the odd appearance of the art room was as real the second time I saw it as the first.

And though I now knew that the bulk of the art pieces on display were copies done by the child genius, that didn't dim the sparkle of the décor in the least.

Actually, the chandeliers were literally sparkling—but he couldn't have made those himself, could he?

"Sorry I'm a lousy host. I'm horrible at making tea and stuff like that. You'll have to content yourself with a relaxing look at my legs."

Um, looking at your legs doesn't exactly make me feel relaxed—insanely jealous is more like it.

Anyway, if I was going to drink tea, I'd prefer the bossman made it—I'd thought the infamous delinquent might be skipping class and spending the day here, too, but apparently (and surprisingly) Fukuroi was paying better attention to his attendance record than I was.

"Damn, I got all sweaty!" Mr. Bare-Legs exclaimed, ripping off his workout clothes.

Once he had stripped down to his boxers, he pulled the familiar redesigned school uniform out of his bag. Geez, he might be a jock, but I wish he wouldn't be so casual about changing in front of a girl.

Still, I couldn't help noticing how beautiful his lightly muscled upper body was, and even more so his legs—

standing there half-naked in the art room, he looked like a real work of art himself.

"I thought everyone treated you like the little brother of the club… But that's not true at all, is it?"

"Little brother? Ah ha ha, yuck. Is that how you thought of me?"

I waited for him to finish changing.

I was divided between wanting to avert my eyes and wanting to watch, but in the end I decided it would seem worse to look away, so I didn't move.

"Um, Mr. Bare-Le… I mean, Ashikaga," I said.

"Just call me Hyota. Or Hyo."

"Oh, okay… Whatever. Um, why did you rescue me…?"

"Helping people is the mission of the Pretty Boy Detective Club!" he answered enthusiastically.

That wasn't what I was getting at.

He seemed like a free spirit—last night, for example, he'd played in the ocean the whole time and barely taken part in the star search at all—but he was evidently also a proud member of the club.

"Get the details from Nagahirolicon, okay? I just did what he said. He told me to go get you, just in case. I swear, that guy orders us around like he's Mr. Important or something."

"Huh… So it was Sakiguchi."

Leaving aside the fact that Mr. Bare-Legs' nickname

for the older student went a little too far for an affection-ate dig, I wasn't altogether surprised to hear that Sakigu-chi was arranging things behind the scenes.

I suddenly felt much more curious about his "theo-ry"—I didn't know what it had to do with the adults who were shadowing me, but the obvious inference was that the two things were somehow linked.

"I already texted him, so I'm sure he'll show up during break. You can ask him about it then," Mr. Bare-Legs said as he finished changing.

I wasn't sure what to think about the fact that his school uniform revealed more leg than his workout shorts.

"Well, for now why don't you just tell big sis what you do know, Hyota?"

"Quit nagging me about it. Anyway, I'm the type who'd rather have big sis teach me a few tender lessons than the other way around. Just wait half an hour. 'What, are you one of those people who rushes off to buy a new clock the second the hands stop moving?' Ah ha ha, do you like my Michi impression?" he asked, looking at the grandfather clock they'd set up in the art room—I was still getting used to Fukuroi's weird metaphors, though, so his joke fell a little flat.

Well, Mr. Bare-Legs didn't seem like the type who would be good at explaining things anyway... And get-ting in a tizzy about it wouldn't help much. Might as well wait for Sakiguchi to explain everything in that lovely voice of his.

I sat down on the sofa feeling slightly let down—but ahh, that sofa *was* comfortable.

I was on the verge of nodding off when it struck me that no self-respecting girl would let herself fall asleep in a room alone with a guy—especially when the guy was this angel.

"So, how did it go with your ever-so-strict parents, Doji? Did you convince them?" Mr. Bare-Legs asked, interrupting my thoughts.

Apparently he was kind enough to worry about me, at least on that front.

"Not exactly... But they did extend the deadline. Mostly they just seemed worn out by my antics..."

"Yeah? Interesting, interesting. So you're a good girl."

"?"

I didn't know what he meant, but I did know he wasn't complimenting me, which made me suspicious—one of my crappiest personality traits is that I'll still get mad at someone, even if they're my savior or my benefactor.

Oblivious to my hostility, Mr. Bare-Legs sat down on the sofa across from me in the same position he'd been in the day before—that is, upside-down, with his legs propped on the back, which strictly speaking doesn't even qualify as "sitting." Come on, stop trying to look up my skirt.

How could he be so boldly lecherous?

Whatever, he couldn't see up it anyway—and at the moment, I was more bothered by what he had said.

"What do you mean, a good girl?"

"Oh, nothing. I was just thinking that I'd never keep a promise like that. I'd shred it without a second thought."

"…"

"It's my life, and I don't like my parents telling me what to do with it, you know? I want to decide for myself. I mean, Nagahiro says his parents chose his fiancée without asking him, but he's head over heels for that first-grader."

Okay, no need to dig any deeper into the first-grade fiancée story.

"It's not like you signed a contract with them or something. You don't have to be so conscientious about their silly deadlines. If you want to spend the rest of your life chasing your dream of being an astronaut, you should. Just like I'm going to spend the rest of my life wearing shorts."

I didn't like having my dream compared to his shorts—but then, his commitment and determination were probably way stronger than my own.

"You know, my parents got divorced a few years back. Let's see, I think it was when I was around ten," he said casually, as if the fact had just occurred to him. "Lots of people said they felt sorry for kids whose parents split up, but I wasn't sure I liked that kind of comment. I mean, people only say that because everyone sort of looks down on the children of single parents. I'd understand if they said it was a pain in the butt for us kids, but..." Mr. Bare-Legs went on, laughing nonchalantly—as upbeat as if he'd just made a funny joke.

I didn't know what to say.

He had a point, but I didn't think the issue was quite so cut and dried—this was heavy stuff for a fourteen-year-old to think about.

But he'd had to think it through when he was ten.

"What I mean is, I didn't want them to use me as a pretext for such an important decision. Whether they got divorced or not, I wanted them to make that decision themselves—and it's the same with you. If you're going to give up your dream, unless you give it up on your own, I feel sorry for your mom and dad—oh, wait, I mean it'll be a pain in the butt for them."

"..."

This angel had a sharp tongue hidden behind his sweet smile.

I'd been somehow assuming I was the unilateral victim in the power dynamic between parents and child—but as he'd just pointed out, that wasn't really the case.

A dream you can give up isn't much of a dream—if you really believe in your dream, it will come true.

Wise words.

But only for the winners.

A loser would say something different.

They would say they lost out by believing in their dream, that they were glad they gave up when they did. Can I honestly say I'm not using the promise I made to my parents as a pretext for abandoning my dream of being an astronaut, when the truth is that I want to escape all the work and hassle involved in such an overblown pursuit?

"What I don't really understand is, why are your mom and dad against your dream of becoming an astronaut? Seems to me like the kind of dream most parents would want to get behind."

"Sure… But it's definitely a dream that's out of touch with reality. It's just as insanely tenuous and insecure as saying you want to be a musician or a manga artist. Don't most parents want their kids to be something like an office worker or a civil servant?"

As a fourteen-year-old, I could hardly speak for how my parents might feel, but that was what I said.

"Hmm. I'm guessing that's somehow connected with the reason you blow a fuse when people mention your eyes?"

I was totally unnerved by his penetrating question—considering what the leader of the club was like, I'd assumed all the Pretty Boys were lousy at logical reasoning and observation, but this kid was sharp.

He'd noticed how much it affected me when Sotoin mentioned my eyes—crap, I guess he wasn't just looking up my skirt after all.

Be pretty.

Be a boy.

And—be a detective, huh.

"Connected? Those two things? Not at all."

"Oh, okay."

I'd nervously braced myself for him to press the point, but Mr. Bare-Legs just left it at that.

13. Together Again

The bell signaling the end of first period rang—and three more members of the club gathered in the art room.

Nagahiro the Orator. Sosaku the Artiste. Michiru the Epicure.

The councilman came in first, then the chairman, and after another minute or two the bossman—I'm not sure of the exact reason behind their staggered arrival, but given the uproar that would rock the school if word got out about these three celebrities (four, including Hyota the Adonis) hanging out, it certainly seemed like a good idea.

To say nothing of the fact that the four of them belonged to the infamous Pretty Boy Detective Club—add that in, and I felt like I was keeping a secret I never wanted to discover in the first place.

Maybe that was the real reason why they swore their clients to secrecy.

The responsibility was crushing.

"You okay, kid?"

Surprisingly, the first words out of Fukuroi's mouth were ones of concern.

Maybe this bad boy wasn't as bad as I—as everyone—thought he was...

A feeling of affinity bubbled up inside me at the thought that maybe he was misunderstood because of his scary looks.

Which is why I overcame my self-consciousness and stuck out my arms in my own poor version of a double fist pump.

"Doin' awesome!" I exclaimed, attempting to put on a brave front. But doing something I wasn't used to at a moment like that was a mistake.

"Idiot," Fukuroi shot back. "What's so awesome about a middle school student being chased around by a bunch of adults? What, you did an awesome job of being chased? Stop bullshitting. What, are you one of those people who says, 'They claim youth crime is increasing, but in fact both the number and severity of cases are steadily on the decline?' Who the hell even says 'youth crime is increasing' anymore in the first place?"

No one does satire like the original.

Also, even as he was bitching me out, he was still concerned for me.

His sincerity made me feel guilty for joking around.

Why am I like that?

"I-I'm fine. I mean, Hyota came to my rescue. And

I'm sure those people couldn't have been that danger-ous... Right?"

"No, they were pretty bad."

My supposed savior wasn't exactly backing me up here.

Mr. Bare-Legs was still sitting upside down, but his smile had vanished.

"I've been kidnapped three times, and the criminals who did it didn't have anything on the people chasing you. They were dangerous, alright."

"You've been kidnapped three times?"

That definitely sounded more dangerous than what had happened to me.

How was he even still alive? But that aside, the back-story did give his words more weight. Not that I needed convincing—we'd definitely been in a hairy situation that morning (and I have plenty of hair to start with).

I was simply trying not to think about the mysterious adults, because the more I did, the more scared I felt.

I needed to relax, so I turned to Fukuroi.

"Make some tea, will you?"

"You sure are getting cheeky... But okay, fine. Anyone else want some?"

Adonis, Orator, and Artiste all raised their hands.

Popular little café he's got going here.

Although strictly speaking, the Adonis raised a leg and the Artiste just raised a single finger—there's something hard-boiled about that child genius.

Speaking of which, their leader was nowhere to be seen.

I figured he was going to come in a little after the others to keep up the staggered arrivals, but it was getting too late for that—the break between first and second periods isn't that long.

If even the child genius, who apparently couldn't care less about me, had shown up, why wasn't the all-important (indeed indispensable) president here?

"Hmm? Ah, the leader? It's elementary, my dear Dojima. He's our Kogoro. He'll be here after school."

"Kogoro?"

Of course he meant Kogoro Akechi, ace detective of Edogawa Rampo's Boy Detective Club novels.

I'd assumed that was where the name of the club came from—but then, shouldn't the leader be playing the role of Kogoro's young assistant Kobayashi, not the adult Akechi himself?

Well, maybe they meant it in the sense that the star performer takes the stage last. There seems to be a surprising rule that the greater the detective's ability, the fewer appearances he inevitably makes in the story—and that doesn't just go for Kogoro Akechi.

Of course, if you ask me, Sotoin's ability in that department is highly suspect.

"Yes. So you'll just have to make do with us until

school gets out."

Oh, that was perfectly adequate.

In fact, I'd feel just fine if the leader never showed up at all.

He could retire right now for all I care.

As I was thinking about that, Michiru the Epicure pulled over a little cart loaded with tea and cookies, just like a proper waiter.

Speaking of which, lots of people know that the Gourmet Club—the fancy restaurant in the legendary *Oishinbo*—got its name from the Gourmet Club run by Rosanjin Kitaoji, the model for the character of Yuzan Kaibara. But actually, *that* restaurant apparently got its name from a story called "The Gourmet Club" written by Junichiro Tanizaki.

It's a vivid illustration of the power of literature—although I bet Edogawa Rampo never in his wildest dreams imagined that the name of *his* famous series would one day be adopted by a loony bunch like this.

"Ptooey!"

"Seriously, that's enough out of you! Stop spitting out everything I serve you! Can't you even swallow a cup of tea without a problem? I was happy about it the first time, but now I'm getting pissed!"

So he was happy the first time...

His face really is hard to read.

Anyway, thanks to the delicious cup of tea and the

circle of familiar faces, I was finally able to calm down—although before last night, I'd never have imagined that being surrounded by these four guys would calm me down.

In fact, just last night I'd withered completely.

Having relaxed a bit, I recounted the morning's events to the four of them—how I managed to obtain an extension from my parents, how a mob of ten-ish mysterious adults chased me on my way to school, and how Mr. Bare-Legs saved me. I kept the part about the full-frontal hug secret.

"I see. It looks as though my worst forebodings were unfortunately right on the money. You should be safe as long as you're inside the school, but…" Sakiguchi trailed off.

Even tinged with anxiety, a beautiful voice is a beautiful voice.

Since the vice president was the one who dispatched Mr. Bare-Legs to intercept me on my way to school, he must have expected the situation to unfold as it did, but he definitely seemed to have been hoping things would turn out differently.

"I don't get it. All Dojima did was look at some stars, so why are those weirdos after her?"

Fukuroi voiced the question in my head.

Why? Why was this happening?

It was like he said—what crazy idea could have

motivated them to chase a mere middle school student like me around? No matter how I wracked my brains, the only explanation I could come up with was the conceited notion that they chased me purely because I'm just that: a girl in middle school.

But even if that were the case, I couldn't conceive of a whole pack of stalkers following someone around unless she was on TV or something.

Or maybe the motive wasn't what I should be puzzling over?

If I took a cue from the Pretty Boy Detective Club and viewed this as a mystery story, maybe the question wasn't whydunnit but rather cui bono—in other words, not why was the crime committed, but who stood to benefit from it?

I had no idea about that either.

Seems unlikely anyone would benefit from chasing around a grouch like me.

"Your personality has nothing to do with it," Fukuroi broke in, without any irony this time.

Apparently he wasn't going to contradict my claim that I was a grouch.

But he wasn't done.

"Nagahiro, you knew this was going to happen from the start?" he asked Sakiguchi menacingly.

He seemed to be implying that if he knew, he should never have left me alone—well, in hindsight he might have a point, but still, I could hardly have brought a guy home with me after being out all night.

"When we let her off the helicopter, it never occurred to me that the situation would develop this rapidly. I only realized how dangerous things had become after I began investigating—in the course of looking into the events of ten years ago, Yubiwa and I discovered the terrible truth."

The terrible truth?

Today's events seemed plenty strange and terrible… But the events of ten years ago? Did he mean my family vacation?

"Yes. I'll explain everything, so please hear me out."

Nagahiro the Orator stood up and tied back his hair in a ponytail as if he were about to address a large crowd—looking far more like a famous detective than the president ever did.

14. The Vice President Solves the Puzzle

"Ladies and gentlemen, gather round!

"Rest assured, I never expected it to come to this—but nor can I say I was entirely without suspicion when Ms. Dojima first brought her case to us.

"Please allow me to recount my tale from the beginning. I expect I will need to repeat several of the points that you heard from Ms. Dojima last night, and for that I beg your kind indulgence.

"Thank you, Hyota, for the applause. But please listen quietly. And with utmost seriousness. Clapping with one's feet creates a disagreeable atmosphere.

"To search for a star.

"As our leader stated, it was a most beautiful request. My boy's heart could not help but pound at the mere mention of it—I suspect that even those of you with no interest in the heavens must have entertained the idea once or twice in your life:

"To find your very own star, and to name it yourself.

"Could a boy have any more cherished desire than to find a star all his own—and to name it after the one he loves?

"No, my girlfriend in the first grade has nothing to do with this. Please be quiet, Hyota. Your next comment will earn you a penalty.

"Simply put, my point is this: the beautiful request to search for a star appeared tailor-made for us, yet at the same time, it has been the deeply held wish of all humankind down through the ages.

"For ten years, Ms. Dojima could not find the star.

"This is understandable. A new star is not found every day—all the more so by someone like Ms. Dojima, who is self-taught and altogether without formal knowledge, blindly groping at the sky.

"Yet people around the world constantly observe the heavens—and astronomers, scholars, professionals, and amateurs all discuss their findings in a free exchange of scientific thought. They may not discover new stars every day, but they do discover them with some regularity.

"The universe is always being watched.

"Always surveilled.

"To put it another way, the 'search for a star' that Ms. Dojima promised her parents she would abandon could more aptly be called an immense undertaking aided by a million allies—and yet, in the course of ten years, they failed to find this star.

"Whatever could this mean?

"Yes, Michiru, the most obvious interpretation of the facts does indeed suggest that the star never existed in the first place—that it was a mere figment of the four-year-old Ms. Dojima's imagination. But if our leader were here, he would surely say that this interpretation is not at all beautiful, and with that, it would be quite properly discarded.

"And with all due respect, I am in full agreement with him. We would be poor detectives indeed if we rejected the statement from a witness simply because she was four years old at the time.

"No, I am not suggesting that we accept it simply because she was four years old at the time. Hyota, that's a one-stroke penalty for you.

"And please don't take him so seriously, Ms. Dojima. I can guess your thoughts, but to be looked at like that by a female student cuts me to the core.

"In any case, how shall we interpret the facts?

"A moment ago, I stated that the universe is under constant surveillance, but that phrase contains an error— can you tell me what it is?

"Our leader's words this morning contained a hint.

"Yes indeed, I am referring to his statement that astronomical observation takes place largely at night—and so, the universe is surveilled in an astronomical sense not constantly, but instead for only half of each day.

"Of course I am speaking only in generalities—as the

leader said, the sun and the moon can indeed be observed during the day as well.

"During lunar and solar eclipses and the like.

"I myself went to observe the recent annular solar eclipse—Hm? With whom? That doesn't matter, does it?

"Yes, yes, I went with my fiancée. Do you have a problem with that?

"Yes, of course, our parents arranged the trip without consulting us. On that point, you are correct. Hyota, two-stroke penalty.

"No, Michiru, I do not need your satire at this juncture. Let's stop this nonsense, that metaphor is not for public consumption.

"Returning to the topic at hand—the theory I devised is this: Ms. Dojima must have seen the star not at night, but during the daytime."

15. Astronomical Observation (Daytime)

During the daytime.

When I heard Sakiguchi's words, half of me thought, "That's ridiculous," but the other half felt like all my memories were clicking satisfyingly into place—yes. Yes, that's it.

I was sure of it.

Commonsense wisdom says you look at the stars at night, so up till now I'd gone with that assumption—but if someone asked me whether I was sure it was nighttime when I saw that star across the sea ten years ago, I couldn't give an unequivocal yes.

To start with, I was a four-year-old child.

That's not an age group big on nighttime activities— would a kid who got sleepy by nine really have managed to look up at the night sky for very long?

It had struck me as risky when I saw Mr. Bare-Legs playing down by the shore the previous night, and he's a first-year middle school student—it's hard to believe that a four-year-old would be allowed to do the same.

Did I see that star—during the daytime?

It wasn't so much my judgment he'd called into question as the whole context of the problem... So did all this mean that it didn't matter whether I was on the school roof or the beach, I'd been off target simply by searching for the star at night?

If I was off target like that for ten full years, I've got to be the biggest idiot in the world...

"It's a nice theory," Fukuroi began slowly. "Not bad, if you're trying to solve a riddle or something. But think about it. Sure, you'll have way fewer competitors if you're observing the sky during the day... But isn't that just because you can't see anything unless there's an eclipse?"

He had a point. Such a good point it might undermine the whole theory—hard to observe much of anything under the bright rays of the sun.

"True enough. It would be difficult to see anything other than the sun itself, or the moon, since it's so close to Earth," Sakiguchi replied.

"And another thing. Even if there isn't much competition in the daytime, there's gotta be some—I mean, nighttime in Japan isn't nighttime everywhere. If Dojima saw her new star during the daytime in Japan but it was nighttime in another country, wouldn't that mean someone else was bound to be observing that same sky? Of course, I don't know much about angles and latitude and longitude and all that hard stuff…"

"No, it's an excellent point. But it depends on *where* you think space begins."

"Where you think space begins?"

"Yes—depending on your definition, altitudes reachable by planes as well as rockets can be considered part of space. You could even argue that as soon as you're beyond the gravitational pull of the Earth and into the zero-gravity zone, that's outer space."

Huh?

This conversation was getting complicated.

In terms of not understanding the hard stuff, there wasn't much difference between Fukuroi and me—and actually, in terms of scholastic ability, he probably had me beat. He may be the delinquent problem-child bossman, but he's in class A, and I'm in class B.

Come to think of it, all the members of the Pretty Boy Detective Club were in class A… Was this some kind of elite group?

Not Sotoin, though. Definitely not Sotoin.

"Simply put, what all of this means is that if the star Ms. Dojima saw was extremely close to the Earth, the angle of its elevation would render it invisible outside Japan—and just as the moon is visible during the day, the proximity of this star to Earth would have made it visible during the day as well."

He was actually pushing the limits of logic with that argument, but the flowing eloquence of Nagahiro the Orator made it sound persuasive.

At the very least, I had to admit he had an interesting point.

"Huh. So you're talking about an object at extremely close range. Like how you can see meteors falling even during the day. Does that mean the thing Doji saw was a meteor? She mistook a meteor that burned up in the atmosphere for a star?"

"At last you've introduced a reasonable idea, Hyota. However, when an object enters the atmosphere from outer space, it will likely be visible around the world during its descent, even if it ultimately lands in Japan. You are right, however, to suggest that the object in question burned up," Sakiguchi pronounced.

Maybe I'm slow to catch on, but I still wasn't picking up what he was putting down—what on Earth was the master orator hinting at?

Or maybe his conclusion was hard for him to vocalize precisely because he was such a master orator—what if his theory had led him to a conclusion he was afraid to state because of the shock it would cause me?

"Sakiguchi," I said.

I was still overwhelmed by the fact that an ordinary student like me was talking at such close range to the boy who'd won the student council election three years in a row.

"I appreciate your thoughtfulness. But I want you to know you can speak frankly to me—I'm ready."

Leaving aside quibbles over definitions, if the star I saw was at an altitude generally not considered part of outer space, then it probably wasn't a star.

It probably wasn't the kind of thing a person should build her dreams on—dreams about visiting that star, dreams about one day becoming an astronaut.

I had understood that much.

Whatever conclusion the Pretty Boys had reached as the result of their detective work, I was ready for the fact that it wasn't going to be good news for me.

Somehow, I'd made a mistake—I was sure of it.

I'd made a mistake, and wasted ten years of my life.

I was determined not to blame that mistake on Saki-guchi—and not on the other members of the Pretty Boy Detective Club, either.

No matter what their conclusion was, no matter how they'd reached it.

I would take responsibility for my own mistakes.

"So please, tell me what you've learned. I want to know—what did I see that day?"

I'd screwed up my courage to deliver that line, but Sakiguchi still hesitated. Finally, he answered in a grave tone.

"A satellite."

A satellite—oh, okay, that was all.

Even though I was disappointed, that ever-so-realistic word also made me feel like I'd been set free, abruptly and cleanly. But before I'd even had a moment to let that feeling sink in, Sakiguchi went on.

"But not just any satellite."

At this point, the child genius—aka Sosaku the Artiste, creator of beauty aka Sosaku Yubiwa—who so far had remained silent just as he had the day before, spoke up for the first time.

"A military satellite."

16. Space War

He said the words so clearly and loudly you'd never guess he almost never talked. There was no way I'd misheard him, but all the same, I couldn't help doubting my ears—a military satellite?

Generally speaking, those weren't the kinds of words that cropped up in a middle school coming-of-age story—although that was probably just my dull perspective on the contemporary world talking. The fact is, those words pop up all over the place these days.

In a sense, this was reality.

The military and warfare don't exist in a separate realm from everyday life—I learned that in social studies class.

Still, it was all so sudden—just a minute ago, we'd all been talking about searching for a star.

We were supposed to be in the middle of an embarrassing, childish story about a girl with her head in the clouds. Why was I suddenly confronting a technical term that I didn't even know how to react to?

Even Mr. Bare-Legs the jokester and the satirical delinquent seemed tongue-tied—while Yubiwa, apparently feeling his role was over now that he'd delivered that explosive announcement, went back to being the silent artist.

An oppressive mood filled the art room—and unsurprisingly, it was the boy with the eloquent voice who relieved it.

Even if he was grateful to the younger student—his co-investigator—for saying what he himself had struggled to say, he must also have been caught off guard. He cleared his throat.

"I'll tell you one thing," he began. "The incident itself is over—it's a fully told, fully resolved story that has nothing to do with us—make no mistake about that… You can listen at your ease."

Honestly, I felt far from reassured—no matter what a master orator he was, no matter how beautiful or eloquent his voice, there was a limit to how supportive he could be. I was grateful for his consideration, but I could do without the prelude—I just wanted him to get to the point. He must have guessed my feelings, because the next thing he said was, "I'll be brief."

Then: "Imagine if you will that a certain private military company independently and secretly launched a military satellite—nothing they planned to use immediately, mind you, this was simply the testing stage, the preparatory stage. Of course, it would have been difficult to hide the launch itself, so they carefully disguised it, inventing a false purpose for their satellite, and only then releasing it—"

Sakiguchi was such a good speaker that he made it sound as if he'd been there himself—but the fact that he and Yubiwa had found out so much not just since the day before but that morning alone was a sure sign of their ability as investigators.

That was somewhat reassuring—*but what if that wasn't the whole story?*

What if there was another reason he and Yubiwa had discovered the truth so quickly?

As I thought about that possibility, the terror I was feeling spread throughout my body—no, calm down.

At least hear him out.

Listen to his summary of this story that's already over—this story from the grown-up world that has nothing to do with young boys and girls in middle school.

"Not exactly a peaceful story. But the development of weapons and military equipment isn't necessarily illegal in itself, is it? I mean, if they got permission first," Fukuroi said gravely.

At first he'd been struck dumb just like me, but as befits the bossman, he was quick to regain his composure.

"Yes, of course. The problem is that they did it without permission—that was what made their activities so shady."

Shady was an understatement—this story was so dark I felt terrified just thinking about it. Maybe my idyllic, simplistic middle school student's mind was to blame, but didn't the secret launch of a military satellite essentially mean they were preparing for war? This story didn't contain even a hint of romantic outer-space adventure.

"Indeed, it was a frightening incident that could not be ignored—and that is why their project came to a screeching halt."

"A screeching halt?"

Fukuroi furrowed his brows at this vague phrase.

"It was shot down—and that too, was kept from the public," Sakiguchi clarified.

"... So, a military satellite was launched and then shot down? Sounds more like starting a war than preparing for one to me. Space war—we're talking about a space war."

Mr. Bare-Legs' comments were light-hearted, but he looked bored—and given how smiley he usually was, that made it seem like the most worthless event in the world.

True enough, this was completely unconnected to the guilty excitement the word "space war" would usually evoke—it was a plain old power game.

"Oh!"

Just then, I had a belated realization.

"So, the star I saw... was actually *the flash of the mil...*

the satellite... being shot down?"

I'm not sure if I hesitated to say the word "military satellite" because I'm a peacenik or a coward.

Anyway, in response to my question, late as it was in coming, Sakiguchi nodded gently. "Yes, I believe that's what happened."

If he hadn't explained everything in that clear, persuasive voice, I might have felt even more upset.

I mean, even if I had almost given up on finding the star, this was still a shock—honestly, a shock big enough to make the world in front of my eyes go black.

Ten years ago, a little girl had seen a glittering star on a family vacation—and dreamt of growing up to become an astronaut so that one day she could fly to that star herself.

But what that little girl really saw was a military satellite being shot down. This was beyond tragic—it was utterly surreal.

"In the end, the private military company was crushed before its ambitions could be realized—so naturally, it was never able to launch another satellite, and consequently, Ms. Dojima never again saw a satellite being shot down—and they all lived happily ever after, I suppose," Sakiguchi said, as if he were wrapping up his tale—but Fukuroi interrupted him.

"Just wait a second now, Nagahiro. You can't keep secrets at this stage in the game. If that stuff really happened, even ten years ago, there's no way we wouldn't have heard about it. When a military satellite gets launched without permission and then shot down, that leaves a mark on history any way you slice it."

It was an obvious objection.

Forget about ignorant old me—if Fukuroi the satirist hadn't heard about it, that was odd. After all, the launch might have been kept secret, but the downing?

Could that have been kept secret, too?

"That reminds me, Nagahiro, you still haven't told us who shot it down," Mr. Bare-Legs interjected.

Good point.

I'd been vaguely assuming that the violence of the "evil private military company" must have been countered by a "defender of justice." But war isn't usually that simplistic.

It's a power game.

"Are you trying to tell us—that the satellite was shot down by a foreign army, then covered up to keep it from turning into an international incident?" Fukuroi piled on. He probably thought he was going pretty deep with that one, but he was still in the shallows.

If that was all there was to the story, then by now the facts would probably have been trumpeted to the world.

But if there was something on top of that—or rather, underneath it… Crap, I really do hate my gloomy-as-India-ink personality at times like this. Actually, there's not a moment in my life that I don't hate it; my mind just keeps going to darker and darker places.

What if it wasn't just the people who launched the satellite?

What if the people who shot it down had a reason to keep things secret, too? I didn't want to consider the worst possible ending to this story, but my mind went there of its own accord, like it was mechanically trooping down the most logical path.

Yes—if the flash of light I saw was a man-made satellite being shot down...

The normal interpretation would be that the flash came from equipment burning up as it entered the Earth's atmosphere—but if that wasn't the case—if I'd literally witnessed the instant that a military satellite was shot down?

If my eyes had seen the satellite exploding—

"What? That would be weird, Doji. Even if the satellite was flying at extremely close range, it still had to be in space, right? For a man-made satellite to stay up, it has to be in the zero-gravity zone—in other words, where there isn't any oxygen. And like we learned in elementary school, if there's no oxygen, things can't burn—"

The truth seemed to dawn on Mr. Bare-Legs even as he spoke.

We sure didn't learn the next part in elementary school.

There's one kind of combustion that can take place regardless of trifling factors like the lack of oxygen in outer space: *nuclear fusion*.

If a nuclear missile shot down the satellite—that couldn't be made public.

This went way beyond a mere military satellite. Way beyond an international incident, and way beyond ordinary violence. This was an act of outrageous destruction with the power to overturn the world order.

"...Nevertheless, it was still most likely a test. In short, if a group of people illegally launched a military satellite, they couldn't very well complain when it was experimentally shot down using illegal means, so someone must have decided it would be possible to keep the whole incident secret. And they largely succeeded in doing so—everything was brought to an end as if it had never even happened, and no one was any the wiser."

"Come on Nagahiro," burst out Fukuroi, "you're trying to force a tidy ending on things—you figured it out easily enough, didn't you? You and Sosaku."

"You're right, and that might be the biggest problem of all," Sakiguchi admitted. "*Anyone could figure it out if they looked into it*—I wouldn't say it was easy, and we couldn't have done it without Sosaku's perseverance, but anyone with the intuition to put together scattered fragments of information would be able to reach the same conclusion we did—and that's what's so dangerous.

"Under the right set of circumstances, anyone could uncover that explosive secret—that's why a witness to the original event spurred on by such circumstances would be considered extremely dangerous."

A witness spurred on by circumstance.

It goes without saying—he was talking about me.

17. Witness

What the hell?

This whole time, I'd been calling the bizarre members of the Pretty Boy Detective Club dangerous characters, but never in a million years could I have imagined that I might turn out to be the real dangerous character—it sounded like a bad joke, but there was no denying that I'd been chased by a pack of mysterious adults that very morning.

Who were they, anyway?

I still didn't know.

But if the flash of light I saw in the sky ten years ago had such fiendish implications, I could understand why some grown-ups might want to chase after me like that.

At the very least, it was a much more convincing explanation than my allure as a middle school girl.

According to Mr. Bare-Legs, those adults were as dangerous as his kidnappers.

When I thought about that, I belatedly realized how

really, truly lucky I'd been to escape them this morning.

But why now…?

I saw that star ten whole years ago.

It was ancient history, wasn't it?

"I'm afraid we must take some responsibility for that—there is no question that our trip with you to the beach somehow triggered the subsequent events."

Sakiguchi sounded genuinely regretful—and I realized he was right. That must have been the cause, or at least one of the factors.

But the flip side was that regardless of that morning's events, they'd been watching me all along—maybe for ten years.

The whole time I was missing the mark with my stargazing, they'd had a bead on me—and finally, for the first time on my last night, I'd grazed the truth with the help of the Pretty Boy Detective Club.

That—was the trigger.

"In that case, it might have been better not to run this morning. Maybe you should have feigned ignorance, pretended like you didn't notice anyone following you, and gone to school like normal."

Although his tone was casual, Mr. Bare-Legs' point was sharp and unsparing—he was right. I shouldn't have let them know I saw them, and I shouldn't have run.

I should have acted stubbornly natural, stubbornly spacey—but since I ran, they'd marshalled their forces and chased me in a pack, which meant that we'd both admitted we were aware of the other.

We'd taken the first step.

And now we couldn't turn back.

"...What's going to happen to me?"

Would I be kidnapped... Or, disappeared?

No way. That kind of stuff only happens in movies.

But the truth went beyond a movie.

I'd unwittingly witnessed something that could never be made public—so whatever happened to me, whatever they did to me, it wouldn't be surprising.

"What's going to happen to me?" I repeated. Pitiful.

Why, when I was normally so prone to bluffing and balking and bullheaded behavior, did I have to sound so imploring at a time like this—or to be more accurate, so servile?

What did I want them to protect?

These guys had no real ties to me.

Even worse, the reason I asked them to take on my case in the first place was that I wanted to take out my bad feelings on them and drag them into my situation—I couldn't forget that.

"Stop obsessing," Fukuroi said.

Figures. A rude brush-off was about all I deserv—

"We've got your back, so nothing's gonna happen to you."

"Huh?"

"Am I wrong, Nagahiro? Doesn't matter who we're dealing with, that's who we are, right?"

"...Yes indeed."

Sakiguchi, who had looked very serious up to that point, finally smiled.

That same reliable smile the student council president always gave.

"It doesn't matter what the adults are up to—we're boys."

Mr. Bare-Legs and even the child genius returned his smile with their own—what was with these people?

How could they smile at a time like this?

The Pretty Boy Detective Club.

I guess they really were different from people like me after all—special characters who did everything on a grand scale. As usual, my lousy personality led my mind down that self-lacerating path.

But at the same time, I couldn't help it—I was happy.

Happy they had my back.

Happy they were on my side.

I smiled, too, in spite of myself.

This was no time to smile, but I couldn't resist—boy, am I ever a creepy girl.

"...Realistically speaking, should we contact the police, tell them I was chased around and almost kidnapped by some suspicious people?"

When my brain finally started working again, that

was what I came up with.

"I wonder. Given the circumstances, the police may well be on their side," mused Sakiguchi, who had finally sat back down on the sofa and asked Fukuroi for another cup of tea.

"Even if they aren't, they'd probably just laugh at us anyway—I highly doubt they'd believe that ten years ago, you witnessed a military satellite being shot down by a nuclear missile."

Fukuroi added hot water to the teapot with a practiced hand before continuing.

"It's not like we have proof, right? All we have is your testimony—and the only people who care much about that are those shady characters connected to the incident... Though if you actually were kidnapped or went missing, then the police would probably treat it as a crime.

"Of course that won't happen," he added. Maybe because of his delinquent background, he came off as oddly familiar with the way police organizations operate.

But it wasn't just him.

The same went for Mr. Bare-Legs, Sakiguchi, and the child genius.

I suddenly began to wonder what sort of cases they'd been involved in in the past—cases of this scale were almost certainly rare, but maybe not entirely novel for them.

...I doubted they kept case files or anything like that.

Since every one of them had such a strong personality, no one really fit the role of the narrator.

As I was lost in those idiotic thoughts, Mr. Bare-Legs made a suggestion.

"If we don't have evidence, why not make some? We might not be able to prove what happened ten years ago, but the incident this morning was real enough, right?"

"Y-Yeah," I stammered.

I felt scared just remembering it.

But how would that constitute proof of anything?

He could talk all he wanted about fabricating evidence, but it's not like the chase that morning left any traces...

"If we were to capture one of *them*, that would be living evidence, right? The people who chased you this morning probably weren't involved in the original incident, but they might eventually lead us to the big boss, like a line of dominoes."

"Wow..." I blurted out.

The concept was simple, but he was thinking outside the box.

It hadn't occurred to me to try capturing a member of the gang that was trying to capture me—he had an angel's appearance, which made him an appropriate mascot, and he had those powerful legs, which made him ideal as a rapid response unit, but apparently he also played a role in planning.

"If they're gonna get slammed for chasing after middle school girls, I bet they'll spill the truth quick. Heh heh heh."

… And he was wicked.

But I suppose what he said was true.

Crimes might not be rankable, but some are rankly offensive.

"Isn't that right, Nagahiro?"

"I'll thank you not to seek my agreement on the subject of the Lolita complex. That has nothing to do with me—and as for the idea itself, it's smart but dangerous. We can naturally expect them to be wary of being followed in turn—and they may be armed."

Armed…

I could hardly imagine them carrying handguns, but even that wasn't guaranteed. I mean, terrifying words like "nuclear missile" were already being thrown around.

The worst-case scenario was entirely possible.

I wanted to believe they wouldn't take my life—but when weapons were involved, that could be the outcome whether they intended it or not.

"Then leave it to me," Fukuroi said quietly as he finished setting our cups of tea on the table. "Violence is my area of expertise. That's why I'm here, right?"

I shivered—his words might be reassuring, but if I was going to take them that way, it meant accepting that he was all too well versed in that world.

More than fear, I sensed danger.

Destructive, degenerate.

A far cry from beauty.

Those lines seemed made to order for Michiru Fukuroi, the legendary delinquent, but somehow, I felt unwilling to accept them. There was an awkward pause. I couldn't help letting my feelings show on my face.

I was powerless and helpless, unable to do anything.

"No, you're here because you cook delicious food."

Just then, the president of the Pretty Boy Detective Club, Manabu Sotoin, gracefully pushed open the door to the art room.

"Fear not, lads. I have a plan."

18. The Plan

They said Sotoin wouldn't be coming until school let out, but his premature arrival instantly relaxed the atmosphere in the art room—he seemed both out of place, and precisely the savior they'd been hoping for.

A moment later, the second period bell rang.

Break was over.

"Alrighty then, those of you in the good boy group, go to your classes. If you run, you probably won't be marked late. The bad boy group will move ahead with my secret plan."

His total lack of hesitation in directing the troops despite arriving after everyone else was just what one would expect from a leader. Sakiguchi and Fukuroi stood up.

I wasn't surprised that Sakiguchi belonged to the good boy group, but Fukuroi?

And Mr. Bare-Legs and the child genius were apparently the bad boys? I had no idea what kind of value system we were working with.

I was in a panic trying to figure out which group I belonged to, when Sotoin interrupted my thoughts.

"Since you're at the center of all this, young Dojima, I'll need you to stay here regardless of whether you're good or bad."

That left, me, him, Mr. Bare-Legs, and the child genius together in the art room.

With this switch-up, the atmosphere in the room did a total one-eighty...

Leaving aside the taciturn Yubiwa, Sotoin and Mr. Bare-Legs were both cheerful, or more frankly speaking, shameless flirts, which lightened the mood.

"S-Sotoin... Did you hear what happened?"

"Ha ha ha, don't worry. I caught the gist."

Had he been lurking outside the door this whole time?

In my opinion, eavesdropping isn't beautiful, but anyway...

"You're talking about Nagahiro's Lolita complex, right?"

"You didn't catch anything!"

All he picked up was the irrelevant nonsense.

"Anyway, I got here as fast as I could. It'd be a big help if you could fill me in," he said, with surprising humility.

Of course, I didn't have Sakiguchi's eloquence, but I did my best to sum up the morning's events for him—which made me realize just what a preposterous story it was. Very impressive that Sakiguchi was able to lay it all out with a straight face.

"Hmmm. So there's no new star after all—what a pity," he said sulkily, pouting with genuine disappointment.

You could call his reaction childish, but the way he clung to the idea of the new star and refused to let go of our original goal even after hearing about military satellites and all that struck me as something else.

Boyish, maybe?

No, a kind of aesthetic.

Manabu the Aesthete—apparently, his nickname didn't simply come from the character it shared with his first name.

In any case, his reaction made me suddenly interested in his "secret plan"—just what kind of idea was this guy, who proclaimed his eye was trained but not his mind, planning to unveil?

Of course, part of me just wanted to watch the sideshow…

"Don't worry about a thing, I'm not planning anything out of the ordinary. Doing things just to be different might be showy, but it's certainly not beautiful. Basically, I'm going to follow the strategy Hyota suggested—capturing one of the mysterious grown-ups who chased young Dojima around to use as a living piece of evidence is a clever plan indeed."

"Heh heh heh."

Mr. Bare-Legs didn't seem to mind the compliment—he was quite the docile fellow when the leader was around.

That, or he was just a wolf in sheep's clothing.

"B-But the problem isn't that simple, is it? The enemy will probably be prepared for us to take that approach... Even if I act as a decoy," I pointed out.

"Decoy? Never. That would be aesthetically unpleasing," Sotoin answered. "My idea is the reverse—*we'll make them lose track of you*. Once they go into a panic, having lost sight of their target, namely young Mayumi Dojima here, we'll press in."

Huh. It was a proper plan.

So proper I felt deflated—but the problem was how to escape their watch.

They knew where I lived, they definitely knew where I went to school, and I'm sure they were monitoring both the front and back gates so closely not even an ant could get past unnoticed. Thanks to the school security staff, they probably wouldn't actually come on campus... But that meant I wouldn't be able to leave even after school let out.

"Ah ha ha. You could live here in the art room for a while, if you wanted!"

Mr. Bare-Legs was right: I'd be comfortable enough in the art room with its canopied bed—actually, I'd probably be more comfortable than in my own home.

It even came with an in-house chef.

The only hard part would be trying not to spit out everything he cooked.

"Hmph. Just who do you think we are?" Sotoin asked smugly.

I felt shut in on all sides—he was supposed to be my ally, but that face made me furious.

I give up, who?

"Fear not, we are the Pretty Boy Detective Club. And the third rule of the Pretty Boy Detective Club is—Be a detective. Now tell me, young Dojima, what is a detective?"

I give up, what?

"What but a master of disguise, of course! The famous Sherlock Holmes was such an expert in that art, he managed to transform himself into an old woman despite his impressive stature."

That was definitely my cue to poke holes in his ridiculous notions.

He'd look like the Fist of the North Star by the time I was through.

I mean, shouldn't he be talking about Kogoro Akechi? Wait, did Kogoro Akechi disguise himself too…?

"Fine, I'll concede that detectives are masters of disguise, but so what? Are you planning to disguise yourself?"

"That point hardly requires a concession, but fine,

forget about that. I'm not the one who needs to disguise himself in this situation—why are you talking as if none of this concerns you, young Dojima? You are obviously the one who'll be putting on a disguise."

"M-Me?"

"Yes, you. You will disguise yourself and slip past the people who are shadowing you. Sosaku, your moment in the spotlight has come!" he cried, snapping his fingers— at which Yubiwa sprang up as though he'd been waiting for this signal.

Sosaku the Artiste.

"Do her up."

Yubiwa nodded in response to this concise command.

I was getting done up?

19. The Costume Artist

I got done up.

"Th-That's ... me?"

I stood in a daze in front of the full-length mirror they'd brought out.

I'd never seen this person who seemed to have escaped the pages of a picture book before, and would probably never see them again. Looking back at me from the mirror was a gorgeous—pretty boy.

Technically all he'd done was put a short wig and a boy's school uniform on me—but I looked like a completely different person.

Having finished his work, Sosaku the Artiste was standing next to me, looking satisfied for once.

Of course he looked satisfied.

Strictly speaking, there wasn't a spot on my body he hadn't worked on, from making up my face, plucking my eyebrows, lacing me into a tight corset, and accessorizing me to fixing up my skin and nails.

The truth is, he'd as good as seen me naked, touched all the so-called "delicate" parts of my hair and body, and generally smashed to smithereens my feminine dignity, but I have to admit that all in all, being handled like a piece of art by a creative genius wasn't so bad.

I was such an honest-to-goodness, full-fledged pretty boy that I was at a loss for words.

"Didn't you say you hate beautiful people?"

The joking voice of Mr. Bare-Legs—who had been exiled to the supply room while this new me was being created—brought me back to reality.

"I-I do. I detest them. Ugh, this is awful. How could he do this to me? I feel like shattering this mirror right now. But my life is on the line, so I'll put up with it just for today. And Yubiwa, can you write down how you did the makeup for me by tomorrow?"

I couldn't keep up my stubborn act.

It was impossible to stay a nasty girl in the body of a pretty boy.

They say beauty is only skin deep, but I felt like I'd shed more than my old appearance.

"He had good material to work with. I could tell how attractive you were from the start," Mr. Bare-Legs remarked.

Seriously?

As far as I could tell you were mainly looking up my skirt...

"Ideally, though, you should show some leg. Those slacks ought to be cut off just below the crotch, so the pockets show below the cuffs."

Give me a break.

Why would I wear shorts when I'm dressed up as a guy if I don't even wear them as a girl? And don't give me advice while you're fixing your wedgie.

Seems Sosaku the Artiste's nickname might also refer to the costume artists they have on TV shows and what not. He had everything he needed for a disguise or costume on hand, right down to the shoes—I guess Sotoin wasn't exaggerating when he said detectives are masters of disguise.

I looked in the mirror again. It was so old and ornate it could have been hanging in a museum, but the pretty boy reflected in its surface was entirely worthy of it. I wanted to stare at him forever.

The word narcissist comes from the story of Narcissus, who was so taken with his own reflection in the water that he dove in and drowned. Like him, I wanted to dive into that mirror.

But if I did, the glass would break!

The image of the pretty boy would shatter—what a paradox!

Setting aside this display of narcissism reminiscent of a certain someone, which was making me want to hurl myself body and soul into the mirror... I really had been transformed into someone else.

No one who saw this pretty boy would guess he was Mayumi Dojima—I could swagger right off campus without fear of discovery.

I was just thinking that we should be able to catch my mysterious shadowers off guard exactly like we'd planned, when—

"This won't do! It won't do at all!" Sotoin shouted.

I realized he was standing behind me with arms crossed, scowling.

"Huh…? Wh-What won't do, Sotoin?"

I glanced back in surprise.

What could his complaint be about this ravaging beauty? If he found fault with this boy's pretty face, then he'd have to take it up with me—wait, this boy *was* me.

Instead of addressing me in my completely confused state, Sotoin turned to Yubiwa.

"He's too beautiful, Sosaku! As I always say, your excessive skill is your greatest beauty and your only fault. You need to learn how to rein in your unbridled talent a little," he chided, rebuking the artist.

What kind of rebuke was that?

In any case, it fell on deaf ears—Yubiwa apparently had no interest in anything other than the pursuit of art.

No one had any respect for the leader.

"What exactly do you mean, Mr. President?" Mr. Bare-Legs asked.

"I told you!"

Now he sounded annoyed.

The leader really did seem to be at his wit's end this time.

"It would be bad enough if he were an oddball pretty boy like the rest of us, but for such a perfect specimen of pretty-boyhood to leave school without a girl at his side would be unnatural. I mean, far from blending in, he'll attract even more attention because everyone will be wondering why such a gorgeous boy doesn't have a girl with him."

I was inexpressibly happy to learn that Sotoin was aware he and his fellow club members were all oddballs, but that aside, he had a good point.

The ordinary me would have laughed off his comment as ridiculous, but in my current state, captivated as I was by his (my) beauty, I could hardly argue with him.

If this boy were to walk home alone or in a group of only boys, he would definitely raise suspicions that something was afoot.

But what could we do about it?

I couldn't pull one of my few female friends into this mess—they'd probably walk home with me if I asked, but I'd be putting them at risk, which wasn't something I could do just like that.

All the more so if it was a girl I *wasn't* friends with.

At the same time, one of the rules of the Pretty Boy

Detective Club was "Be a boy"—so I didn't think any girls belonged to it.

"Oh dear, it can't be helped. It is the duty of the leader to make up for the overly excellent work of his members. I'll put my skin in this game."

Apparently he meant that literally, because with that, he began to pull off his uniform.

"Duty calls. Once more, if you please, Sosaku!"

20. The Perfect Couple

School was over.

The ravishing girl and the raving beauty of a boy left Yubiwa Academy Middle School together—the raving beauty, of course, was me, and I'm sorry to say the ravishing girl was Sotoin.

We were the work of a true artist.

Broadly speaking, Sotoin too had simply put on a wig and a girl's uniform—and while the transformation wasn't as dramatic as mine, the result was nevertheless perfect.

In this case, the materials really were excellent.

And the disguise made the most of those materials.

She—I mean he—no, I do mean she—was no ordinary beauty—she radiated an extraordinary elegance. She made that unremarkable uniform with its run-of-the-mill design look like a fancy dress. Even her standard-issue stockings did more than simply hide her legs.

The results were so perfect that they completely

upended the simple, obvious thought that if anyone was going to dress up as a girl it ought to be Mr. Bare-Legs.

If this gorgeous masterpiece had been created by anyone other than the child genius, they probably would have considered their career as an artist complete.

...By the way, I tried casually suggesting that Mr. Bare-Legs play the girl's role, but he refused to wear women's clothing. Since his face looks so feminine anyway, I thought he'd take on the job willingly, but my best guess is that he's experienced some kind of trauma that he won't talk about.

In any case, we decided that since they'd already seen his face, it might not be a good idea for him to accompany me, even in disguise.

But...

"...I know it's become de rigueur to dress up as a girl in these series, but you're the first one to do it in the very first volume."

"Hm? Did you say something?"

Nope, not a word.

Accurately speaking, it was Yubiwa, not Sotoin, who was the master of disguise, and while Sotoin looked perfect, he had no acting skills whatsoever—which is to say, he did nothing to change the tone or register of his voice.

Though neither did I, for that matter.

But he did "walk in beauty like the night," as the poem goes—and since he's so short, the height difference between us was perfect for a middle school couple.

Very casually, and without being clingy, he took my arm.

Imagine, a guy linking arms with me!

Actually, he did it so naturally and with such class that I didn't feel anything like that at all. I fought back the urge to shake him off, telling myself that a gentleman would never push away a girl who took his arm like that.

Although I wasn't a gentleman to start with…

So many roles were reversed (along with Mayumi and Sotoin).

After Sotoin's makeover was complete, I was able to see how we looked next to one another, and in the course of waiting for school to let out (in the end, I skipped all my classes along with the members of the bad boy group) I'd gotten used to the situation well enough to assess it more calmly, at which point I'd started to worry that we still stood out too much.

Or rather, stuck out—like a pair of sore thumbs.

We weren't quite like Holmes in his old-lady costume, but if a perfect couple like us walked home from school together, forget about the people tailing me, we'd be the talk of the whole school.

"Who *are* those two?" they'd all be saying.

The more I thought about it, the faster I wanted to walk, but I had to keep pace with Sotoin, who was holding onto my arm.

A gentleman must always match the pace of the lady he is escorting—uh, not exactly.

Anyway, Sotoin and I left the school campus—and from that point on, I really started to get nervous, since anyone could be watching us from anywhere.

All I knew for sure was that the members of the Pretty Boy Detective Club were supposed to be watching from behind—Yubiwa, Sakiguchi, Fukuroi, and Mr. Bare-Legs were in position to follow the followers.

They were armed with sketches of the people who had chased me that morning, which Yubiwa had drawn based on descriptions from Mr. Bare-Legs and me.

Yubiwa kept his mouth shut and made himself invisible in the art room, but I was starting to suspect he possessed the best detective skills of them all—honestly, it sort of felt like a waste of his talents, but on the other hand, it also felt as if he was the perfect man for the job.

By the way, when Fukuroi came back to the art room at the end of the day, he took one look at my transformed self and said, "Looks like they did a number on you. Learn to say no, kid."

No metaphors, no satire, just a straightforward comment.

"Just because you're putting on a disguise doesn't mean you have to go all the way to dressing as a guy."

True enough.

But the artiste had a vision.

"Shit, you're putting me in a tight corner, looking like that."

I didn't really understand what he meant, but I decided to take it as a compliment. The fact that he didn't say anything about Sotoin made me think this probably wasn't the first time the members of the Pretty Boy Detective Club were seeing their leader in drag.

Although Mr. Bare-Legs didn't miss the opportunity to zing Sakiguchi by saying, "That's probably what your girlfriend is gonna look like in the future."

I hate to say it, but I was starting to get curious.

What kind of first grader was this girl?

If she was going to look like this in the future, she sounded like a fairly promising fiancée—anyway, without hurrying, but without pausing, either, we started walking away from school.

It was hardly the time to be thinking about this stuff, but walking around in public dressed up as a different person felt weird, and kind of fun.

Seriously, though, this was not the time or place.

This wasn't a game—we were in real danger.

Not just me, but Sotoin, too.

"…Hey, Sotoin, can I ask you a question?"

"As long as it's a beautiful question."

Come on, what kind of an answer is that?

I had no idea if my question was beautiful or not, but

I asked it anyway.

"Why are you going this far for me?"

I'd asked Fukuroi a similar question the night before, but with a totally different meaning—I'd asked him (with plenty of irony) how serious the Pretty Boy Detective Club was.

I didn't need to ask that question anymore.

At this point, I could hardly doubt their seriousness.

All the cross-dressing made me feel like we were in some kind of ridiculous skit, but still, they wouldn't have gone this far if they weren't serious about helping me.

That's exactly why I asked Sotoin the question I did.

Why was he taking this so seriously?

"Whatever the truth ends up being, we know now that the star I spent ten years searching for doesn't exist. You called my case beautiful, but it's actually impossible to fulfill. Risk is the only thing left for you guys now… So wouldn't it be smarter for the Pretty Boy Detective Club to withdraw?"

"Hmm, I hadn't thought of that, but it certainly would be the smart thing to do," Sotoin said, clapping his hands.

Seriously, what kind of detective wouldn't think of that?

He said his mind was untrained, but it seemed like the problem was that he simply didn't use it very much.

And then, without thinking any more about it, the unthinking detective said, "But it wouldn't be beautiful"—

promptly rejecting my sensible idea.

"…"

"It goes against my aesthetic. Fear not, young Dojima. We don't protect our clients' confidentiality, but we do protect our clients."

Um, please protect my confidentiality, too.

How am I supposed to trust a bunch of bigmouths?

Hearing this pretty boy, that is, pretty girl's words, an indescribable feeling washed over me—I felt embarrassed, or rather, pathetic.

No matter how nicely they did me up as a pretty boy on the surface, I was still the same old me on the inside.

Looks are just looks.

I'm a servile, nasty, gloomy contrarian—

"Kind of like Cinderella."

"Huh?"

"You know what they say: The fairy godmother dresses Cinderella up, then at the ball the prince falls in love with her at first sight, and then he finds her using the glass slipper she left behind—she's a passive princess who doesn't do anything for herself."

What the hell? Not only was I calling myself a princess, I was saying this to a guy who was kind of a princess himself.

"I disagree," Sotoin replied. "She deserved to be rewarded for putting up with that mean stepmother of hers for so long. It would be crazy if she *weren't* re-warded."

I'd brought up the fairytale just to vent, but his response was surprisingly serious.

"It's the same with you. Those ten years you spent searching for a star were definitely not wasted—and we, who met you because of your search, will definitely not let them go to waste. You will be rewarded. Even if that star does not exist."

" ... "

I knew he wasn't saying all of this to make me feel better—he didn't have that sort of sensitivity.

These were his true feelings.

And he was truly serious about what he said.

"Incidentally, while we're on the subject of Cinderella, some people wonder why the glass slipper didn't disappear at midnight along with the ballgown and the pumpkin carriage, but if you ask me, that's the most ridiculous question in the world."

"R-Really? I've always wondered about that myself."

I suppose it isn't so much an inconsistency as the sort of expedient plot line that traditional stories often have—but the aesthete's answer was different.

And sharper.

"Clearly it was part of the fairy godmother's lovely plan from the start! If Cinderella were only rewarded for the beautiful determination that led her to crash that fancy ball at the castle with surface decorations like a pretty dress and a carriage, that wouldn't be very impressive magic, now, would it?"

21. The Strategy Fails

Sotoin was accepting risk without reward—but the real risk didn't fall to him, or even to me, but rather to the four boys in the rear guard who were preparing to capture the people tailing me.

When you get right down to it, all Sotoin and I had to do was safely slip through their net. Meanwhile, the other club members were in immeasurable danger because they had to come into direct contact with the mysterious adults.

Of course, they really only had to capture one of them—and Fukuroi had said that shouldn't be too hard, even for some middle school boys, since they would outnumber the adults four to one.

"We'll target the one who looks weakest, so we'll be fine," the student council president added with the bearing of a military advisor.

That reassured me a bit... But I still couldn't help worrying.

For his part, Sotoin didn't seem very concerned at all, although I'm not sure if that was because he trusted the other club members or because he just wasn't thinking about it.

Anyhow, the perfect pretty-boy-pretty-girl couple in disguise had slipped past the net—or so it seemed.

We still couldn't let down our guard, but I figured I could at least breathe a sigh of relief since we were quite a distance from school and yet the people shadowing me were nowhere to be seen.

"Hmm, I wonder…"

Sotoin sounded a little disappointed—don't tell me he was hoping for trouble!

"But really, young Dojima, you must be quite sensitive to the world around you. Most people wouldn't know if they were being followed or not. I, for one, would have no idea."

This was a bit of a problematic statement for a detective—although I got what he was trying to say.

"Uh huh… Girls are more sensitive to that stuff than guys."

"Is that so? I suppose that also explains why you were able to see the satellite being shot down—most people wouldn't be able to see something like that even if they tried. I think we'd better start considering admitting girls to the Pretty Boy Detective Club. We are always looking for new members, but so far, we've never had a girl join.

We would have to adjust Rule #2, but gender discrimination is unacceptable in this day and age anyway."

"Ah ha ha…"

If they publicized the names of the current members and made an official recruitment call, I bet they'd be flooded with applicants—although I doubt many would meet Sotoin's exacting aesthetic vision.

Which reminds me of those glasses I forgot this morning… If I went home looking like this, my parents would probably be surprised… I'd promised them…

"Oh no!"

I stopped short in the midst of these scattered thoughts.

Sotoin, who was still holding my arm, stumbled forward and gave me a look that said, "Whatever is the matter?"

"Let's take a different—"

But it was too late.

It wasn't the people tailing me.

In a sense, it was even worse—I'd spotted a pack of boys from a nearby middle school heading straight for us.

As for what was so bad, well, the boys and girls from that school and ours don't exactly get along—to put it mildly.

I figured things wouldn't get too nasty since we had Fukuroi-the-bossman to glare them down, but both sides take their territory very seriously—and we'd gotten so wrapped up in slipping through the enemy's net that we seemed to have accidentally crossed into the buffer zone.

Normally I wouldn't worry so much about that—but a beautiful couple like this was just asking for trouble.

What the hell.

Here we were talking about military satellites and space war, and suddenly a childish turf battle rears its head…

Needless to say, I didn't have the kind of worldly experience necessary to dodge a fight with kids from another school, and I highly doubted Sotoin did, either—in fact, I was afraid his unvarnished honesty would only throw fuel on the fire.

Even if it didn't come to that, what the hell would happen if they found out I was a girl dressed up as a guy, or that Sotoin was a guy dressed up as a girl—

But at the very moment when the kid who appeared to be the leader of the group noticed us and opened his mouth to shout something, a figure stepped between us.

The timing was too perfect to call a coincidence—clearly, it was all too intentional.

The interloper, who seemed to have sensed the explosive tension between our two groups and stepped in to prevent it from erupting, was a tall woman dressed in a dark suit. The kids from the other school clicked their tongues like their fun had just been spoiled, and passed peacefully by.

It was incredible.

Rescuing a couple in trouble would have been an impressive enough show of skill on its own, but to rescue them before the trouble even started—

"Ahh, beautiful," Sotoin exclaimed candidly.

He was always candid when it came to his opinions on beauty.

Skill aside, the woman herself was gorgeous—I wasn't sure about her face since she was wearing sunglasses, but the rest of her looked like a fashion model.

Not only was she herself stylish, but even her clothes seemed more attractive because she was wearing them.

"Th-Thanks… You really saved us," I managed, since whatever was going on, her actions deserved proper appreciation. I stepped toward her, thinking about how I always had a hard time expressing my appreciation to the members of the Pretty Boy Detective Club, but I'd expect the words to come out more smoothly with a member of the same sex, when—

"No worries. I was first in line anyway," she said, taking off her sunglasses.

And then I blacked out.

Apparently, I'm incapable of expressing my gratitude.

22. The Twenties

When I came to, I was inside a car.

It took me a second to realize that's where I was, though—because my surroundings were totally different from what a person normally imagines when they hear the phrase "inside a car."

To start with, it was very spacious, with cushioned seats facing each other and even an extravagant minibar off to one side... I hate to make judgments based solely on stuff I've seen in foreign movies, but... with evidence this clear, I had to presume I was inside a limousine.

A limousine.

One of those fancy automobiles that are so long you wonder how they manage to turn corners.

I doubt I was unconscious for all that long, but my surroundings had changed completely... What had happened? What had been done to me?

I tried to move and failed.

Someone was holding my arm in place—an incredibly beautiful girl.

Which is to say, Sotoin.

His eyes were closed and he seemed to be asleep—but he was gripping my arm fiercely.

"The kid is unconscious, but he won't let go of you—that's some fighting spirit, if you want to call it that."

The voice was coming from directly in front of me.

I looked up in surprise.

I was sure no one had been in that seat the last time I looked—but now, even though I'd only looked away for a second, the lady from before was sitting there with her long legs crossed.

She was even more beautiful without her sunglasses.

She'd taken her suit jacket off, too, revealing a low-cut pink blouse—it was open to the third button, which was located around the level of her breasts, boldly exposing them.

I was impressed that she nevertheless managed not to look trashy, but this was no time to be spellbound by her beauty.

"He's a brave one, eh? From what I could tell from the pat-down, he is a boy, yes?"

"…"

The question was so unexpected I couldn't muster an answer—naturally, she must have patted me down, too, and realized that I was a girl.

Or more accurately, she must have already figured

out what was going on and then kidnapped us because of it—but why?

I wasn't wearing any old disguise—this was the superhuman work of Sosaku Yubiwa, the child genius with the resources of no ordinary middle school student at his fingertips.

I messed up by letting my guard down when she rescued us from the approaching gang of kids, but still, I doubted anyone would be able to see through Yubiwa's disguise so easily.

"Here you go, young lady. You'll be needing these, I believe."

With that, she nonchalantly held out a pair of glasses—but a shiver went down my back.

They were the very glasses I'd left on the bathroom sink that morning.

In other words, this woman had somehow managed to break into my house—and that wasn't all.

" . . ."

"What? You don't need them? In that case, I'll toss them out the window," she teased.

I gave in and reached out my arm—the one Sotoin wasn't holding on to.

Surprisingly, she handed them right over, and I put them on.

"Heheh."

She smiled bewitchingly.

It was a beautiful smile, but it reeked of superiority, which didn't sit well with me—after all, she was the kidnapper, and I was her prisoner.

Obviously, a hierarchy was at work here.

... Still, I hadn't been handcuffed or gagged, which as a prisoner was really more than I could have hoped for.

"..."

"Hmm? You'd like to say something? Ah, you want to know my name? I'm Rei. I think our acquaintance will be brief, but it's a pleasure nonetheless."

Although I hadn't asked, she—Rei—told me her name.

Judging from the bold way she said it, you'd never guess she was a shady character—although that could hardly be her real name.

"Oh, don't take that the wrong way. When I say I think our acquaintance will be brief, I don't mean I'm going to do something to you two—I abhor violence. I gave you a little neck massage when I wanted the pleasure of your company in the car, but that doesn't really count as violence, does it? We're in charge of pickups and dropoffs, which means our job is simply to deliver you."

She just kept on answering questions I hadn't asked.

Even accounting for the fact that I'm the type who lets my thoughts show on my face, she was a bit too responsive.

"Of course, I don't know what they plan to do with

you after I drop you off—would you like something to drink? No? I see. Then I'll take the liberty of having one myself."

Rei took a bottle and glass from the minibar—she seemed to be kicking back, acting as if her task of picking us up and dropping us off was already complete.

And she was probably right. It was complete, and she had all the leeway in the world to kick back.

I didn't know where we were headed, but the limousine had been driving nonstop, so we didn't have any opportunities to leap out or anything like that.

Rei hadn't left us unbound out of kindness—she hadn't bound us because there was no need. No matter how spacious the limousine was, I was certain the second either of us tried anything, she would give us another "little neck massage."

Her work wasn't the only thing that was complete.

The whole affair was already over.

"…"

"Hmm? I can't quite read that expression—what are you thinking, Mayumi?" Rei asked with apparent interest, pouring her alcohol into the glass and setting it in the drink holder.

"…I want to talk to the most important person in your organization," I said, desperately trying to steady my shaking voice.

"I'm the most important person in the Twenties. And

also the most competent. Did you have some business with me?" she replied.

Her tone was nonchalant, and she didn't seem to be lying.

"I'll be obedient. I won't resist."

"What, you want to announce your surrender?"

She sighed like she was bored.

"Resist if you want, it doesn't matter. Go ahead and stop being docile. Although Ms. Rei is getting a little hot and bothered hearing that from a pretty boy like you."

"...It doesn't matter where you take me or what you do to me. But this boy..." I said, gesturing to Sotoin. "Please let him go. He has nothing to do with this. I'm begging you... Please don't drag him into it."

"...Oh? You mean it? That's a surprise. I thought you were one of these modern kids who only think about themselves."

For some reason, Rei was talking like she knew me— or was she just reading my face again?

Whatever the basis for her comment, though, she was right.

That's exactly the kind of kid I am.

I only think about myself, and what's more, I hate myself for it—which makes me a completely hopeless case. I'm a warped, servile girl, and I'll definitely be a boring adult when I grow up.

But that's precisely why I didn't want Sotoin getting

pulled into this.

I didn't want him to be dragged down by a girl like me.

Not a pretty boy like him, who maintained his commitment to a beautiful aesthetic even when he was knocked out.

"But why do you think I would go along with a request like that? I'm a criminal, a kidnapper, a bad person. Do you really think I'd respond to a sob story like that?"

"…Yes, I do."

"You do. Why?"

That was a hard question to answer.

My belief had no clear basis, and I hadn't deduced it from anything—but if I had to explain, I'd say it had to do with when she kidnapped us.

Rei had rescued us from a fight with kids from our rival school—and if I asked her why, she'd probably say it was because she was first in line.

But when she saved us, I'm pretty sure she hadn't realized who I was yet.

Most likely it was only after she'd rescued us and saw my eyes close up for the first time that she realized who I was. Because even a genius artist couldn't change my eyeballs.

I didn't think she was a kind person.

She was a kidnapper and a criminal.

But I didn't think she was entirely evil, either—at the

very least, she was kind enough to pause her work to rescue a middle school couple in distress without promise of reward.

… And if that wasn't the case then I was in trouble, because she probably wouldn't agree to let Sotoin go.

"Alright, fine. Do what you want."

She agreed so easily.

She sounded like she couldn't care less.

When I made the offer, I was ready to put my life on the line, so I felt a little let down that she went along so readily, but I suppose that's what they mean by looking a gift horse in the mouth.

Rei turned to the driver.

"Twelve. Stop the car when you have a chance."

Twelve… And earlier she'd called her group the Twenties… So maybe she was named Rei after the Japanese word for zero?

Anyway, just as I was breathing a sigh of relief and letting my mind wander…

"There's no need to stop," Sotoin declared, still gripping my arm. At some point he must have woken up.

As for why he didn't want them to stop…

"That's not a beautiful way to live."

23. Manabu Sotoin

I'd called him an idiot many times up to that point, but finally I was sure of it.

Manabu Sotoin was a genuine idiot.

For the first time in my life, I'd met that rare creature: an irredeemable fool—and I half wished he'd give me back the courage I'd expended in offering my own life to a criminal in exchange for his idiotic freedom.

For now, let's not worry about the question of when he'd woken up—it's enough to know that the idea of sacrificing me to save himself was so contrary to his aesthetic sensibility that he simply couldn't permit it.

But if that was the case, I wish he at least would've played possum until the limousine stopped—not that I think the two of us could have escaped at that point, but I personally wouldn't have squelched the possibility in advance...

Or did playing possum also go against his aesthetic values?

"Well, I didn't mean to, but it looks like I slept well after that late night—I only hope I looked as beautiful as I usually do while I'm asleep. So, I assume you've kidnapped us?" he finished.

He sounded completely undaunted by talking to an adult. Though however brazen he might've been, he was still dressed up as a pretty girl.

Rei sat there as cool as ever with her arms and legs crossed, but a glimmer of confusion showed through in the way she tilted her head.

For someone who prided herself on her quick wit and ability to read people, an idiot like Sotoin—that is, a person whose thought process was impossible to understand—was probably a bad match.

"I'm Manabu Sotoin, president of the Pretty Boy Detective Club."

"...The president. You don't say." Rei gave a provisional nod.

She had an adult attitude, although it would be hard to say she had an adult's composure.

"If you don't mind my asking, what exactly is the Pretty Boy Detective Club?"

She directed her question more at me than at Sotoin—but I wanted to know the same thing.

What *was* the Pretty Boy Detective Club?

"You'll find out for yourself before long—so for now, why don't you share with us your true identity and the goals of your organization."

Where did he get off requesting a confession so brazenly?

"...Our identity is unknown, and our only goal is money."

Rei sounded fed up.

I think she was trying to avoid getting swept up by Sotoin's pace, but by the time she had that thought, it was already too late.

As for me, although I was worried about dragging Sotoin and the others into my personal problems, and from a subjective perspective I deeply regretted having done so, from an objective perspective, I was the one who had been swept up...

"If you want to know who hired us, you might as well give up—I don't know myself. That's how the Twenties protect our clients. All we're doing is bringing this girl to the place we were told to bring her, in the manner we were instructed."

Rei's tone was positively oozing with the desire to let Sotoin out then and there, without any further bargaining or negotiations of any kind.

You don't have to be good at reading faces to pick up on something like that.

"How strange, to protect someone by not knowing anything about them," Sotoin said.

If he was calling you strange, you were done for.

"I prefer to defend people by knowing about them."

"Defend them? You can't defend anything if you're dead, can you?" Rei shot back.

Sotoin didn't flinch at the tacit threat—to the contrary, it seemed to bring him to life.

"You can defend your aesthetic. If you can't do that, you can't defend anything—and understanding aesthetics is the same as understanding everything," he declared definitively.

"...So you understand, then? You know why they're after her?"

"Of course. It's because she saw something she shouldn't have."

He sounded very proud of himself, even though it was the other club members who'd figured that out.

Come to think of it, the leader hadn't done much of anything this whole time...

"If you ask me, military satellites and missiles aren't at all beautiful—although I suppose the vision of them scattering across the sky on the far side of the sea may have been as beautiful as the glittering stars," he said, as if trying to be fair.

...Though, maybe he was right.

No matter how evil the source of that light was, it stole my heart ten years ago, and that truth had never disappeared.

"I do have one question, though. Ultimately, the

information can't be kept secret simply by silencing one girl. Or do you plan to kidnap everyone who saw that flash of light?"

"Ah, so you don't know the truth after all."

Rei looked at me, finally seeming to regain her composure—apparently, she was back to normal now that Sotoin had at last said something sensible.

"*She was the only witness*—which means she's the only one we have to kidnap. The fact is, Mayumi Dojima's were the only eyes in the world capable of seeing that flash of light."

24. Mayumi Dojima

I've got a problem with my eyes.

My eyesight isn't bad—it's too good.

Of course, it depends on how you define good—but basically, my field of vision is configured to a much broader range than the average person's.

If I said I could see radiation and X-rays, we'd be leaving the realm of mystery novels and getting into sci-fi territory, but that's actually not far from the truth. I don't understand all the details myself—the truth is, I never wanted to know, and so I avoided finding out.

In other words.

My eyesight is really, really, really good.

So good I see things I'd rather not see.

Things I'd be better off not seeing.

So good I notice people following me who I don't need to notice.

So good I can see adults hiding around corners and mobs of kids from other schools when they're still far away—and.

So good I witnessed a military satellite being shot down even though the sun was shining, and even though I would have been better off not seeing it—since I guess my eyes could see even farther, back when I was four years old.

That's why I'm the only one.

The only person in the world who knows—the only person who saw it. Or to put it differently, there's no one else in the world who can testify to that satellite being shot down.

That's the situation.

"From the client's perspective, it's an easy job—simply by monitoring Mayumi here, they're able to maintain their margin of safety."

Rei shrugged—as if she'd regained control of the conversation. She did seem like the type who was more suited to explaining things than asking questions.

The question now was how the detective would take this, but Sotoin didn't look particularly satisfied by her explanation—to the contrary I saw him get indignant for the first time.

"So! You people watched secretly for ten years while a little girl who just wanted to chase her dreams searched the sky for a star that didn't exist, hiding the truth from her all the while—I don't like it one bit. When Nagahiro hears about this, he'll be furious!"

"I wasn't the one in charge of that part—but you're right that Mayumi has been under surveillance. Not just since last night, either—for ten years."

Sotoin turned to me.

If he wanted to know whether I ever realized they were watching me, I'd have to say no—having overly good eyesight doesn't mean I have the gift of "clear sight," by which I mean clairvoyance.

But you could also say the reason I became so servile and obsessed with how other people see me is that a part of me did know I was being watched.

"And you 'protect yourself' with those glasses, don't you?" Rei asked jokingly. I could never approach her skill in reading faces.

"I heard they were talking about lifting the surveillance soon—since you were supposed to give up astronomical observation on your fourteenth birthday. But then you got in a helicopter of all things and headed to the beach where you'd first seen the star. Imagine that! And attended by a group of four lovely boys, for the record."

"Four of them?"

The lovely boy—currently dressed up as a girl—whose existence had just been erased from the record appeared puzzled by this statement, but Rei ignored his question.

"That's what led the client to send out the Twenties—honestly, I thought they were being overly cautious. I never guessed you'd get so close to the truth in a single day," she said.

"Hah. *That* is the Pretty Boy Detective Club," Sotoin exclaimed proudly, puffing out his chest—though for the record it really had been the work of *four* lovely boys that got us there.

"No, really, what the hell *is* this Pretty Boy Detective Club?" Rei asked in exasperation.

To me, her inability to completely ignore Sotoin seemed like a sign that she wasn't a bad person at the root—not that she'd let me go or anything like that.

Because even if she wasn't a bad person, she was a businessperson.

"Perhaps you'd like to hear the rules of the club?"

The leader, who didn't excel at reading faces or hearts and was therefore entirely undisturbed by Rei's snide remark, continued to proudly stick out his chest—which looked weirdly suggestive, since when he was being made up as a girl, the artist had paid special attention to his bust.

My guess was he'd completely forgotten what he looked like right then.

"One: be pretty. Two: be a boy. Three: be a detective—"

"And that makes you the Pretty Boy Detective Club? What, you took the name straight from those rules?"

"Wrong. If that were the case, we'd just be some pretty boy detectives—and when a few pretty boy detectives get together, you have nothing more than a gathering of pretty boy detectives. The most important rule of the Pretty Boy Detective Club is the fourth rule."

The fourth rule?

I'd totally assumed the rules or whatever ended with number three… But there was another one?

They were pretty, they were boys, and they were detectives.

What else could there be?

"At the risk of overstating the case, the fourth rule is ultimately the only one we need. The fourth rule of the Pretty Boy Detective Club—"

Sotoin gave a satisfied, exceedingly proud smile.

"Be a team."

I finally got it.

That's what a club is: a team. And the reason he'd been puffing out his chest and acting so proud this whole time despite not doing a single thing himself—was that this whole time, he'd been proud of his team.

"Boss!"

At that moment, the driver called back to Rei.

His voice was tense.

"Something to report—a bicycle has been following us for a while now!"

I didn't need to look out the back window.

The only person who could possibly be riding that bike was the pretty boy with the bare legs.

25. Chase

No one knows exactly how fast a road bike can go. I've heard they can easily keep up with a car, but in the end it comes down to who's riding the bike.

It's hard to imagine anyone maintaining those top speeds for long—even if the bike can theoretically go fifty-five miles an hour, I doubt anyone could really maintain that speed for fifty-five miles.

Basically, chasing a car on a bicycle is an impossible dream.

But Mr. Bare-Legs was making the impossible possible—he was tailing the limousine, standing up as he pedaled without a thought for how he looked.

Maybe he couldn't overtake it, but he didn't let it out of sight—

"Could that be…the same boy you were riding double with this morning in such an odd way?" Rei asked, narrowing her eyes as she watched Mr. Bare-Legs—she hadn't lost her composure, but I'm certain she was surprised, to say the least.

"Bingo. That is Hyota the Adonis, he of the beautiful legs," Sotoin pronounced.

"I see..." Rei looked unexpectedly serious in the face of this introduction.

Was she too stunned to speak?

I mean, no one could laugh at a boy on a road bike barreling straight toward them as if his life depended on it.

To the contrary, the sight of him covered in sweat, pedaling like crazy, was beautiful enough to steal anyone's heart.

Of course, his exposed legs themselves were also beautiful.

"What should I do, Boss? Going that fast, I don't think he'll be able to avoid us if I stop the car suddenly."

Twelve, the driver, glanced anxiously in the rear-view mirror.

"Out of the question! What are you thinking? He's a child," Rei replied, brushing off his suggestion.

"He's not a child, he's a boy—and an exceptionally pretty boy at that."

Rei nodded. "True enough."

It didn't seem like an offhand remark.

"So what do I do, Boss? Even if he doesn't catch up, shaking him off will be tough—and if he follows us the whole way, he'll get in the way of our mission. He sure stands out."

Unlike a certain someone, Rei seemed to command respect from her underlings, and Twelve immediately withdrew his less-than-restrained plan of slamming on the brakes—although I'm sure any driver being chased by Mr. Bare-Legs would feel viscerally terrified.

After all, it *was* strange.

The cutest member of the Pretty Boy Detective Club—the one who looked like a girl even without dressing up as a girl—turned out also to be the most athletic. A limousine attracts plenty of attention on its own, but a limousine being chased by an archangel on a bicycle? That went beyond standing out.

"...Say, Mayumi," Rei said suddenly, still looking out the back window. "How does this situation look to you?"

"Um, what do you mean...?"

Rei ignored my confusion and went on.

"That kid doesn't look like he's chasing us at random, does he? I think he's got a clear goal in mind."

A clear goal...?

Actually, that made sense. He was chasing us so desperately on that road bike, but even if idealism and die-hard spirit allowed him to catch up with us, his prospects beyond that were zilch.

She'd just capture him, too.

Mr. Bare-Legs might be athletic, but he was no match for Rei. She'd effortlessly nabbed Sotoin and me with those slender arms of hers, and she'd do the same to him—and he'd end up getting kidnapped for the fourth time in his life.

Did that mean I should assume he had some other prospect for victory... Or at least some other trick up his sleeve?

I had no idea what it might be, though... Not the faintest clue. I just have good eyes—that doesn't mean I have Rei's outstanding analytical power.

I timidly explained that to her, to which she responded, "You overestimate me. The reason I asked your opinion is that I have no idea myself."

She shrugged, then turned to Sotoin.

"Perhaps the leader might be able to enlighten us?" she asked grudgingly.

"Ha ha ha. I can't do that."

"...I don't like the idea and I'm not eager to do it, but I could torture you until you talked."

"It wouldn't work, because of all the people in the world, I have the least idea of what the boy following us on the bike is planning to do—as leader, I respect the independence of my team members."

"Didn't you say you prefer to defend people by knowing about them?"

"I was talking about clients. My club members aren't so soft that they need my protection."

"I see... And they protect you," Rei said with a satisfied nod.

It may have been the only thing she could feel satisfied about.

"Okay, then let's ask the boy himself. In any case, it's poor form to let someone that conspicuous chase us endlessly—I'd rather ask him directly how he plans to protect this nonsensical leader of his."

"D-Directly…?"

She ignored my surprised reaction and turned to the driver.

"Twelve. Stop the car—but wait till you have enough space, and do it slowly and carefully, making sure you obey all traffic regulations. And put on your hazard lights so you don't cause a collision."

26. The Cell Phone

Mr. Bare-Legs fell flat on his back.

His bike fell apart at the same time.

It seems that chasing a car without so much as a pause to drink water had pushed both the boy with the beautiful legs and his state-of-the-art road bike to the limit… He'd been covering it up with pure determination, but the truth is, if Twelve had kept driving for ten more minutes, he might have shaken him off.

In that sense, Rei gave in not so much to his fighting spirit as to her own curiosity—although "gave in" is a bit of an overstatement.

The battle hadn't even begun.

It all depended on the gambit Mr. Bare-Legs was delivering via bicycle—its nature would determine whether stopping the limousine was a wise decision on Rei's part.

If she'd managed to nip his strategy in the bud…

Of course, it was entirely possible that he had desperately chased after the limousine with no strategy in mind and no chance of winning whatsoever... Although I fervently hoped he would say that wasn't true.

I hoped he would say that, but covered in sweat and gasping for air as he was, he didn't seem capable of saying anything—right then, he was lying on the seat of the limousine where Twelve had set him after retrieving him from the road, and Rei was handing him a bottle of mineral water from the minibar.

Come on, don't let your enemy nurse you like that.

I'm begging you, tell us you've got something up your sleeve.

"Hah...hah...hah...ah ha ha, Mr. President, I'm so glad you're okay..."

The first words out of his mouth as the limousine started to move again were a profession of his concern for Sotoin. Impressive show of loyalty.

"Yes, as you can see," Sotoin replied equably.

Although from what I could see, he wasn't actually okay at all.

"If you're able to talk now, I'd like to request an explanation, Mr. Shorts... I see one boy in drag and another showing off his legs. Does that mean the Pretty Boy Detective Club is some sort of band of hedonistic aesthetes?"

Rei's skeptical question was only natural, but of course that wasn't what she wanted him to explain—she wanted to know what he had in mind by chasing the limousine.

"… I'm the leg ace, sis."

"Leg ace? I can see that."

In contrast to us middle school girls, who were all so terrified of his legs, this thoroughly grown-up woman responded by crossing her own fishnet-stockinged legs as if to make sure we all noticed them.

But for once, Mr. Bare-Legs didn't seem to be boasting about his own fine pair.

"No… Not leg ace… I mean, yes, I'm an ace when it comes to legs, but…" he gasped between breaths. "What I meant to say was 'legate.'"

Legate?

That was quite the archaic term… But I was pretty sure it meant "messenger."

"You are, are you? I thought deliveries were my specialty," Rei replied.

Mr. Bare-Legs withdrew a cell phone from his shorts pocket and handed it to her—leaving aside the fact that cell phones are banned at our school, this one was a clunky flip phone way too bland for the average middle school student.

But when Rei saw it, she turned white and abruptly made a move to stand up. As if to push her back down, Mr. Bare-Legs jabbed the phone at her again.

What was going on?

Leaving me in the dark, Rei finally took the phone without a word. Sotoin, who I figured was as much in the dark as I was, seemed unmoved.

"Hyota, you must be tired. Let me rub your feet," he said instead, tending to his club member.

Why was he so oblivious to danger?

"..."

Rei scrutinized the cell phone, her beautiful face twisted in a grimace—she didn't exactly look displeased, but I could tell things weren't going as she'd planned.

What was with that phone?

"One... No, that can't be right. Two? No, including you, it must be three... Otherwise it wouldn't be an even trade," she considered, probing Mr. Bare-Legs for an answer.

"Right on the money... We've got three of 'em," he answered, as the leader rubbed his feet.

I wasn't sure what to make of this vision of an utterly exhausted, sweat-drenched pretty boy having his feet massaged by an apparent pretty girl—it went beyond aesthetically pleasing to downright licentious... Add in the setting of the limousine, and I felt like I was watching something I shouldn't be.

But what were these "three" they were talking about?

"...Twelve. Whose whereabouts are currently unknown?"

"Well, Number 20 is always impossible to get in touch with—but 13, 18, and 19 have all missed their regular check-ins."

Rei didn't even try to hide her sigh.

"I see. So this isn't just some erotic club—pardon me for treating you like children. But do you understand what that means? For us to treat you like adults?"

Since she said this right after sighing, it didn't come off as threatening—but her matter-of-fact tone made the words feel more real than a threat.

I couldn't really say I understood what she meant, though.

I didn't even understand what the Pretty Boy Detective Club had done—were 13, 18, and 19 members of the Twenties?

The fact that they hadn't checked in must mean—

"*Our strategy succeeded*, Doji—we weren't able to prevent you and the leader from being kidnapped, but we captured some of the people who were following you. Three of them, actually," Mr. Bare-Legs crowed with a mischievous smile. Then, still reclining, he turned to Rei—at just the right angle to peer past her crossed legs and up her skirt.

"So, sis, time for a hostage exchange."

27. Hostage Exchange

So that must be the gambit Hyota the Adonis had delivered via bicycle—they had three of the Twenties captive.

Right, I'd forgotten.

I got flustered when Sotoin and I were kidnapped, but that was the plan to start with.

Interesting—so the strategy itself hadn't failed.

Not only that, while capturing just one of them would have been a huge achievement, they'd managed to capture three… Which meant they weren't asking for the three of us in exchange for one of them, but for an equal exchange of three for three.

The moment the leader disappeared, the competency and efficiency of these middle school students started to shine… Honestly, what kind of a club gets more done when its leader isn't around?

Then, the cell phone Mr. Bare-Legs had put his life on the line and his legs to work in order to deliver must've belonged to one of their three captives… Either 13, 18, or 19.

A cell phone.

I didn't have one, but for adults in today's society, they're the most important piece of personal identification.

Of course, a cell phone used by a criminal organization is sure to have an unbreakable password and every kind of security measure available to keep outsiders from messing with it—as they say, set a thief to catch a thief— but since the Pretty Boys had taken the practical approach of delivering the phone directly to Rei, she couldn't very well ignore it.

Or would she?

Any organization willing to take a job that required kidnapping innocent middle school students constituted a genuine "criminal enterprise"—so I could easily imagine her cruelly abandoning any members who were captured in the line of duty.

If that was the case, then Mr. Bare-Legs had pointlessly thrown himself into the jaws of death—a fool venturing everything to gain nothing.

He'd gone through all that just to have the leader rub his feet.

That would be beyond pitiful.

"And … ?" After a moment, Rei, the boss of the Twenties, prompted him. "How exactly is this hostage negotiation meant to go? Are you suggesting that in exchange for you three, I can get back my three dear team members?"

"Precisely."

It wasn't Mr. Bare-Legs who replied, but Sotoin.

He spoke as if he was in control of the situation, but in fact he was one of the pawns being traded.

He was like a captive princess, with the outfit to match.

I, on the other hand, was a far cry from a princess.

"Our negotiator will be calling that phone any moment now—you can discuss the details with him," Mr. Bare-Legs said, ignoring his leader. "And you can forget about misleading him with your womanly charms—our negotiator isn't interested in girls above the first grade."

"Y-You have a criminal in your club…?"

For a second, Rei let her raw emotions show on her face, but at that very moment the phone in her hand began to vibrate.

The ringer was turned off.

Guess that made sense for someone at work.

But Rei didn't answer it right away—maybe she was afraid to talk to someone with a lolicon?

"19 is calling 13's phone…" she muttered listlessly. "In other words, you're making one of my staff call me? Or perhaps you forced him to tell you the password and your people are calling from his phone? In either case, I don't recall training for a situation where a middle school student forces me to talk."

She stared at the vibrating phone as she analyzed the situation. Her penetrating gaze—the same one she wore when she was reading someone's face—fell onto the number displayed on the small screen.

"Well, it's clear enough that your negotiator is no ordinary guy with a lolicon."

Apparently, the Pretty Boy Detective Club negotiator's Lolita complex was becoming established fact behind his back.

"Hello?"

Finally, Rei stopped analyzing and answered the phone—looking very capable and businesslike as she did.

Though she actually *was* a criminal.

When you think about it, a Lolita complex in itself is more a matter of preference than a crime, so for a real criminal to be calling Sakiguchi a criminal was somewhat unfair.

"Ladies and gentlemen, I am Nagahiro Sakiguchi, vice president of the Pretty Boy Detective Club."

Rei had been kind enough to put the phone on speaker, and the student council president's lovely voice reached all the way to where I was sitting across from her.

The vice president of the Pretty Boy Detective Club.

It was impressive that he could say that with a straight face—and while I couldn't see him through the phone, I was sure he did have a straight face.

He sounded calm.

More worldly than a middle school student—or maybe just wise to this other world.

"I believe you know why I'm calling," he continued.

She also knew about his lolicon.

"I'd like to propose a trade. If I'm not mistaken, our leader, our rapid response officer, and our client are currently enjoying your hospitality—I request an equal exchange of those three for the three gentlemen we are currently looking after."

"Time and place?" Rei asked tersely.

She may have been trying to limit the quantity of information she shared by keeping her response as short as possible, or as a mature woman, she may have wanted to limit the duration of her conversation with a guy with a lolicon as much as possible.

"As for the time, as soon as possible. As for the place, I suggest our middle school. My apologies that you will have to retrace your route."

"That's not a problem—and I hope I don't need to say this, but don't get the authorities involved. Although I suppose we'd both be in trouble if that happened."

"?"

Sakiguchi's mild confusion was readily apparent over the phone—even the brains of the Pretty Boy Detective Club could hardly have expected to be called a criminal by a criminal.

In the end, he seemed to interpret her words to mean

that the pride of an organization calling itself a Detective Club would be injured by looking to the police for help.

"Yes, of course, this negotiation is between our two organizations alone. The Pretty Boy Detective Club and the Twenties," he said finally.

The implication was that he already knew the name of their organization—a sign, I suppose, of his skill as a negotiator.

"This is a businesslike deal with no strings attached— if you give us back our three, we'll ask for nothing more."

"Okay. That's all we want as well—but if you hurt my team, I can't guarantee the safety of these three… Or, to be clear, I'll kill them all," Rei said coldly. "I'll use the cruelest method I can think of. And I'll kill you, too. I have a feeling you're the kind of person that the world and all of humanity would be better off without—it would be the first good deed of my life."

"Hm? Okay…"

Since Sakiguchi didn't understand the second half of her speech, he apparently didn't register its full terror— but to me it seemed that Rei would be true to her word. If something happened to her staff, she'd make sure we paid in full—she wasn't the type to abandon her underlings as per the logic of a criminal organization after all.

Still—she wasn't a good person.

In fact, a villain who cared about her team might be the worst possible person to negotiate with. How fully did Sakiguchi understand that?

"Of course, we've taken the liberty of tying up the prisoners, but we intend them no great harm. We are treating them with as much hospitality and courtesy as possible given the situation. Therefore—"

"That's my line."

I heard a rough voice interrupt Sakiguchi—they must have had the phone on speaker, too. The voice belonged to Fukuroi, although it was so low and threatening I couldn't tell at first.

"Don't act like this doesn't involve you, lady. You're like one of those people who talks about personal responsibility while saying irresponsible things like 'On the other hand, some people might say that anyone who uses that kind of app has to take personal responsibility for the consequences.' Just try touching a hair on Dojima's head… Or the leader's, or Hyota's. I'll do whatever it takes to find you and kill you."

"Forget about that, just get dinner ready. I got kidnapped and missed dinner, so I'm starving. I feel like Chinese tonight," Sotoin said without looking at the phone, as if to curb Fukuroi's threatening attitude—he was still rubbing Mr. Bare-Legs' feet, and I was starting to wonder if he was literally incapable of taking anything seriously.

Honestly, "I feel like Chinese"?

Was the kitchen in the art room that well stocked?

It did make the prospect of returning to school for

the hostage exchange a little more appealing...

"Leader... You sound like your usual self," Fukuroi replied in an exasperated tone—that sounded exactly like his own usual self. At least, as far as I knew what his usual self sounded like.

"That I am. Do I ever not sound like myself?"

No, probably not.

"Mind if we get back to the topic at hand?" Rei cut in.

She wasn't rattled by Fukuroi's fierce words in the least.

"We'll start heading toward the school now. If that's alright with you?"

"Of course. Would you mind calling this phone when you're close? Take care—"

Just as Sakiguchi had regained control of the conversation, Rei hung up on him.

Setting the phone down next to her, she turned to Sotoin.

"You certainly do have a good team, from what I can tell," she said.

"The best there is," he answered.

With that, he finally finished the massage and sat up straight—and when I glanced at Mr. Bare-Legs, I realized he'd drifted off to sleep at some point.

The kid had some nerve... Though unlike the leader, he did have a sense of urgency as well, so I suppose the impudence could be overlooked. Especially since it seemed he hadn't so much fallen asleep because of the massage as gone into a dormant state after using up all his energy.

Fukuroi had told Rei she better not touch a hair on our heads—and while they hadn't hurt me or Sotoin, I was starting to think we'd better get Mr. Bare-Legs some medical attention as quickly as possible.

"Your team doesn't seem so bad either. Or, are they bad? You're a criminal organization, after all," Sotoin mused foolishly. "Anyhow, giving up your mission to save your team is admirable leadership. I don't care for criminality, but that spirit is beautiful, if nothing else."

"And what about you? Are you the kind of leader who could make that decision?"

"Fortunately, none of my people, that is, none of the people under me would ever need me to save them. I specialize entirely in being saved."

Does that specialization even exist?

Do leaders like that even exist?

"Boss, what are you going to do?" Twelve asked from the driver's seat. "You'd never really give up the mission, would you?"

"Never," Rei answered. "However, our opponents naturally will have guessed that we don't plan to give up... And if they honestly plan to complete the hostage exchange like good little children, without alerting the police or attempting to capture us, then they really are a dull crowd."

"We're not good little children. We're boys, and boys will be boys," Sotoin said.

For once he was making a reasonable point.

A once-in-a-century event, I'm sure.

"Tell me, Sotoin," Rei began. "What do you think your team plans to do?"

"Come now. Do you really think I know?"

"Unlikely, I suppose—but you're at least capable of thinking about it, aren't you? If you're going to call your-self a detective, how about at least attempting to deduce what your team members are up to?"

Rei was being exceedingly provocative.

Up until a minute ago, she wasn't exactly ignoring him, but she was definitely not paying him much atten-tion.

Maybe her view of him had changed after she wit-nessed Mr. Bare-Legs, Sakiguchi, and Fukuroi treating him with unexpected fondness—or maybe she had made up her mind that if she had to negotiate with the Pretty Boy Detective Club, she had to properly confront their leader.

This was not what you could call a positive develop-ment.

Although they called themselves detectives, in real-ity the members of the Pretty Boy Detective Club were no more than a bunch of natural-born eccentrics, and the club itself was like a middle-school extracurricular activity. If they were to have any chance against a genuine criminal organization, it would lie in Rei and her associates underestimating them as "just a bunch of kids"—but Mr. Bare-Legs' pursuit and Sakiguchi's negotiation techniques seemed to have convinced her otherwise.

To put a finer point on it, Rei no longer seemed inclined to treat us more kindly because we were children—but Sotoin didn't appear to share my concern in the least.

"I can see how you'd want to know what I've deduced," he replied, sounding almost as though her provocative tone made him happy. "For some reason, everyone always wants to know—what on earth I'm thinking, that is."

Something tells me he was misinterpreting their curiosity.

Seriously, what *was* he thinking?

"Three hostages for three hostages. It sounds like an equal exchange, but I wouldn't say the incidental risk is necessarily the same on both sides—if the negotiation fails, we, the Pretty Boy Detective Club, stand to lose two members and one client, but you, in the worst-case scenario, could see your entire organization fall apart."

To my surprise, Sotoin's thoughts on the matter were relatively sensible—as he said, even if the potential gains were the same for both sides, the potential losses were not.

I hadn't thought about it like that... And even if I

had, I wouldn't have laid it out for Rei so cockily.

I mean, we didn't need to give her a product warning label.

"So if I were in Nagahiro's place, I would spare no effort in winning your trust—in other words, I wouldn't call the police, I wouldn't touch the hostages, and I would assure you an honest deal."

"Sure, that makes sense."

Rei sounded somewhat impressed by Sotoin's analysis—but she also looked puzzled because she couldn't figure out why he was saying all of this to her.

It was no ordinary boy who could explain his thoughts yet leave the listener even more confused—although at the moment, not being ordinary was all he had going for him.

"If I were going to lay a trap, I'd definitely lay it in that very assurance. A moment of carelessness on the part of your organization—or frankly speaking, on your part—becomes Nagahiro's chance, O Rei-vishing Beauty with Twenty Faces."

"Who are you calling a Ravishing Beauty with Twenty Faces?" Rei shot back immediately, shaking her head.

But the "ravishing beauty" part did seem to make an impression.

After all, even the most beautiful women don't often get called that in the course of everyday life…

"Your task, on the other hand, will be to turn the trap

against us—it will be a keen battle of wits demanding all the intelligence we can muster. What a beautiful prospect, don't you agree?"

Rei, who apparently did not agree, shook her head again.

"Well, it's certainly quite an idea," she said, as though she were complimenting him. "And tell me, Sotoin, what's the assurance he'll offer, and what's the trap?"

"Don't ask me."

He had no idea??

If he meant that he didn't know what was going to happen, then as a pawn in this hostage exchange, I wished he hadn't opened his mouth at all. But he just shook his head and kept talking.

"There is one thing I know for sure, however."

One thing he knew for sure? Was he planning to run his mouth even more?

At this point, no one could gain anything from that.

Maybe not even Rei.

"And what might that one thing be?" she asked.

"I'm having Chinese food for dinner tonight."

28. Apology

Rei moved up to the passenger seat.

I guess her conversation with Sotoin was draining her mental energy—or maybe she wanted to avoid getting attached to us as a result of interacting any more than she already had.

Naturally, the doors had automatic locks on them, and couldn't be opened from the inside—Sotoin, the deeply slumbering Mr. Bare-Legs, and I were imprisoned in the back seat of the limo.

Of course, the seat cushions were soft, we had the minibar, and in general the atmosphere was a bit too luxurious to merit the word "imprisoned"—although not surprisingly, since I had no idea what our fate would be a few short hours from now, I found it impossible to relax.

"Look at that, young Dojima. This minibar doesn't just have mineral water, it's got a good selection of nonalcoholic juices, too. Would you like something?"

...Though for the always-relaxed Sotoin, neither the

atmosphere nor our situation seemed to matter.

I wanted to tell him I was in no mood to eat or drink, but I couldn't ignore my body's physiological thirst, so I accepted an orange juice.

"…Sorry I didn't tell you about my eyes," I said after cooling myself down with a drink of the juice (which was tasty, but not so tasty I spit it out). In other words, I apologized.

Finally being able to say sorry lifted a weight from my chest.

Although at the same time, I hated my own personality for only being able to apologize when I was this hard pressed.

"Huh? Your eyes? Oh…"

Sotoin shifted in his seat.

"Don't worry about it. That does explain some things, though. Is that why you got so mad when I complimented you for having beautiful eyes?"

So you noticed when I got mad about that, Mr. President! And knowing that, you continued to relentlessly compliment them anyway!

I was on the verge of yelling at him, but the front and back seats weren't separated by a glass divider.

Rei and Twelve could hear our conversation the whole time, of course, but I didn't want to get too loud and make them think we were horsing around or not being serious back there.

"I can understand getting angry when someone disparages your weaknesses, but what I still don't understand is why you get mad when someone compliments your strength."

"…Strengths and weaknesses are the same sort of thing, aren't they? It's not just me—I think a lot of people hate being called beautiful."

"Do they?"

Sotoin spread his hands like he couldn't comprehend the concept.

Figures.

I'm an overly self-conscious middle school girl, but how can I describe this guy's sense of self? It's not like he's insufficiently self-conscious by contrast, but…

I was fiddling aimlessly with my glasses and pondering this question when he interrupted my thoughts.

"Leaving aside the question of whether or not your eyes are beautiful, they should be an advantage for someone who wants to be an astronaut, right? I mean, what could be better than good eyesight for a job like that?" he asked.

Sharp point—with which he was poking my soft spot.

That was precisely the problem.

Strengths and weaknesses are the same sort of thing.

You can have too much of a good thing.

And sometimes, too much of a good thing is even worse than a bad thing. You can give up because something is bad, it gives you an out, but when it's too good there's no excuse—

"Having good eyesight means my eyes get overused."

"Hmm?"

"My eyes *are* good. I can see people hiding on the other side of a wall—or a military satellite being shot down. But they're a little *too good*."

"Hmm?"

"I've been told that if I push them too hard, I'll go blind by the time I reach my twenties—that's why I usually protect them with these glasses."

That's why I had to give up my dream.

I couldn't dream of being an astronaut, or doing any other job that required me to use my eyes—because I couldn't give up my eyesight in exchange for a dream like that.

How could someone who even had to be careful about using a smartphone dream about the future?

But I hadn't given up yet.

I wasn't making any specific effort to become an astronaut—which in a sense was the same as making an effort to give up my dream.

But I couldn't give it up completely.

I could understand giving something up because I wasn't good enough, but to give up because I was too good—what the hell was what?

It was like being affirmed and rejected in the same

breath.

Praised and crossed off the list.

What sort of a gift was that?

"I see now. So that's why you hate beautiful people. You have a subconscious tendency to dislike people's strengths."

Sotoin gave a satisfied nod, but I think I just plain old hated them—or was he right?

Beautiful voice. Beautiful legs. Beautiful palate. Beautiful art.

I couldn't say part of me didn't resent these guys who so perfectly expressed their talents.

"I understand how you feel. A lot of people resent my beautiful aesthetic, too."

Uh, I think they probably just resent *you*.

Though I must admit, I was wildly jealous of his lack of uncertainty and self-doubt.

"But yes, that does make sense. That's why your parents oppose your dream of becoming an astronaut. And they're right, too."

Hey, stop being so sensible all of a sudden!

C'mon, aren't you going to say something about how their position is correct but it isn't beautiful?

Guess not.

"Boyhood doesn't necessarily overlap with one's rebellious phase."

"Oh, okay…"

The definition of "boy" seemed to be surprisingly complicated.

If my parents' position was so clearly correct that it was clear even to a total oddball like Sotoin, I guess I would have to accept it... But still.

I had mixed feelings about it.

I knew my parents were doing what they did because they cared about me—but the result was that an unbridgeable chasm had opened up in our household.

A family destroyed not by hatred but by love.

That, too, was possible.

But if I accepted their position, wouldn't that mean I couldn't do anything? Giving in to their rightness would be like admitting there was something wrong with me—

"Being a boy means dreaming, but it doesn't necessarily mean never giving up on a dream—you can have as many dreams as you want."

Sotoin laced his hands behind his head and leaned back as he spoke—his girl's outfit only serving to emphasize the fact that it was a somewhat impolite pose.

"Relax, young Dojima. I'm certain finding a dream will be much easier than finding a star."

29. Leading the Way

Flying down the streets with shocking speed, the limousine returned to Yubiwa Academy Middle School—our path was boomeranging back on itself, but a boomerang would never have made it there as quickly as we did. As you'd expect from the guy entrusted with the job of driving the boss of the Twenties around, Twelve was an outstanding driver.

There could hardly be a less suitable place to park a limo than next to a school, but its conspicuous size alone made it an awful choice for criminal activity.

I couldn't understand why Rei would choose such a noticeable vehicle for her crimes, but who knows? Maybe she just hadn't thought about it.

One upside was that they probably weren't pulled over by the police very often—although I could see Rei choosing it just because she liked flashy things.

In any case, we got back to school much faster than I normally would have thought possible—which was clearly part of Rei's strategy.

By speeding up the course of events way beyond what Sakiguchi would be expecting, she robbed him of time to prepare—returning to the back seat, she pulled out 13's cell phone.

I wondered why she was making a point of making the call in front of us, when she could have done it just as easily from the passenger seat—from my inexperienced point of view, I figured maybe she wanted to be able to hand us the phone when the person on the other line asked if we were unharmed.

But on that point, Sakiguchi was one step ahead of her. She may have thought she was taking the lead by calling him, but when she did…

"…I'm sorry, Boss."

A deep voice answered.

A male voice I didn't recognize…

As soon as she heard it, Rei switched off the speakerphone.

Maybe she didn't want us to hear him speaking in that dejected, not-very-cool voice.

I could understand her feelings… I mean, forcing a hostage to handle the negotiations was, well, fairly nasty on Sakiguchi's part.

In the opening skirmish of the negotiations, the Pretty Boy Detective Club had seized the initiative.

"It's fine… Don't worry about it. I'll make them compensate us for this. I'll create an opportunity for them to pay us back, mark my words. Is everything okay? Oh, I didn't mean it that way... I'm asking if you guys are okay. Hmm... But the fact that the kids haven't called in back-up is good news."

Since I couldn't hear the guy on the other end anymore, I had to go by Rei's side of the conversation... But it sounded like ultimately Sakiguchi hadn't called in the police.

They'd said the police would come to our aid if things got rough, but the fact was that once the leader, Mr. Bare-Legs, and I were taken hostage, Sakiguchi couldn't really go to them...

"So what's next? Should I take these three up to the roof of the school? Okay, to the place where Mayumi used to observe the stars? I see... How very fitting. Yes, fine... No, stay on the line."

Rei watched us as she talked to her underling—she was repeating the key points back to him despite having turned off speakerphone not out of consideration for us but probably because she wanted to see how I'd respond, since I was listening so closely.

If Sakiguchi had laid some kind of trap to outwit her, where could it be?—If she found that out, she could use it against him.

"Get out," Rei said, holding the phone to her ear as she climbed out of the limo—Sotoin swung the still-sleeping

Mr. Bare-Legs smoothly onto his back as he complied.

Apparently, he was capable of that sort of moderately gallant, or, almost leaderly act of consideration... I was starting to see why they liked him even if they didn't respect him.

The sight of a pretty girl carrying a pretty boy on her back, on the other hand, had a perverted flavor I couldn't really comment on...

The school at night.

Even though we'd raced back at record speed, the school day was long over, and not a person was present in the halls—it was just the time of day I always used to observe the stars.

At night, I like to look at stars from the roof of the school—at night, I liked to look for stars from the roof of the school.

Maybe the biggest mistake in that sentence has to do with whether or not I truly liked doing it, though.

Even considering that the guards had already gone home, Rei breached the school's security with surprising ease, leaving Twelve in the limo and bringing us with her into the building—I guess the notion that I was safe at school was just another mistaken assumption based on so-called common sense.

When your opponent is a genuine criminal, there is no safe zone.

Not school, not your own home.

"Alright—from this point on, Mayumi, I'll be needing your assistance," Rei said once we were inside the building.

By this point, I wasn't surprised that she knew exactly where I used to go to look at the stars—but, my assistance?

No sooner had she said the word than she plucked my glasses off my nose—and before I could complain, she put her arm around my shoulder and pulled me close.

I highly doubted she planned to win Sakiguchi over by showing him what good friends we'd become—so what could this be about?

"I'll be borrowing your eyes for a while. Those eyes that can see through walls," she explained.

I'm not sure how she did it, but even though her arm was around my shoulder, my head was locked in place so I couldn't move it at all.

"If a trap has been laid, I'd like you to spot it for me. Oh, don't bother saying anything out loud—I can pretty much tell what you're thinking by looking at your face."

"...!"

At that moment, I imagine my face was eloquently communicating my terror—this lady came up with some crazy ideas. She was planning to use my eyes as an infrared camera? Not good.

Why? Well, because Sakiguchi didn't know about my eyes—and therefore any scheme or trap he'd come up with to outwit Rei wouldn't have taken them into account.

He wasn't counting on my overly good eyesight.

Rei had been listening from the passenger seat when I apologized to Sotoin for not telling him about my eyes—which revealed to her that I hadn't been completely open with the Pretty Boy Detective Club.

"Lying clients are part and parcel of the detective trade, of course," Rei sniggered.

So her strategy was already in motion at that point—by moving up front, she was able to eavesdrop on everything I said to Sotoin.

She may have gone along with the hostage exchange negotiations, but she had no intention of abandoning her original mission, which was to kidnap and deliver me to her client—she planned to return to that task as soon as, or, even as she got her three team members back.

Which meant that in a worst-case scenario, not only would she refuse to hand over the three of us, but she might also kidnap the remaining three members of the club... By using—no, misusing—my eyes.

No, even worse—by abusing them.

Taking advantage of my eyesight, which I'd never managed to make use of myself, was a brilliant idea on her part, but horribly depressing for me.

Not only had I failed to be of any use to the people who were trying to help me, I was now actively making their situation worse.

It was awful.

These damned eyes of mine were getting us all up to our eyeballs in trouble.

"…Uhh…"

I wanted to somehow send a signal to Sotoin, who was walking behind me—couldn't I at least help him and Mr. Bare-Legs escape? The ace runner might be surprisingly muscular, but he was still slender and probably not too heavy—Sotoin should be able to run with him on his back.

The fact that Rei was holding onto me so tightly meant she was paying that much less attention to Sotoin—if only he would take this opportunity to run in the other direction.

…Yeah, right.

He'd already thrown away one chance to save himself—he probably wouldn't abandon me now.

Still, I couldn't help thinking that by following along obediently with no strategy whatsoever, he wasn't fulfilling his role as a detective at all.

If he wasn't going to escape, that was fine, as long as he showed some sort of leadership worthy of a leader in the meantime… But even though Sotoin tended to say weird stuff, his actions were surprisingly uneccentric…

"Don't worry, as long as you don't resist, I won't get violent—not toward you, and not toward the kids in the

Pretty Boy Detective Club. Actually, I'm looking forward to meeting them. I'm curious if the guys who call themselves that really are pretty boys."

On that count, she probably wouldn't be disappointed.

"Pretty boys... I might be able to make some cash selling those."

Rei delivered this unfriendly line in a not entirely joking tone.

Wonder if there's a demand for pretty boys with lolicons?—Quite possibly, Rei could read even idiotic thoughts like that on my face.

At this point, all I could do was pray that Sakiguchi had laid a trap so ingenious I wouldn't be able to see through it.

For the moment, I didn't see anything ahead of us or around the corner... But unlike the president, who on top of being irrational was frighteningly rash, the vice president couldn't possibly be engaging in a hostage exchange with no strategy whatsoever.

If he didn't have one, no one did, and we were in trouble...

In any case, as I was pondering these questions—which is to say, as I was completely failing to do anything useful—the four of us had made our way up the empty staircase and arrived in front of the steel door leading to the roof where we'd agreed to make the exchange.

All the while, Rei was talking with her captured team member on the cell phone—not only was she using me as her "eyes," but she seemed to be using the hostages in the same way.

Talk about a right-hand man—she used her underlings to augment all five senses as well.

Criminal organization or not, there could hardly be a more resourceful method of leadership.

"..."

She wouldn't let me close my eyes either, so I looked at the other side of the door—that is, I looked through it.

Very intently.

It's hard to put into words what I saw, and Rei probably knew what I was seeing without my having to put it into words anyway—but if I had to, I'd describe the image as six faint, blurred silhouettes, unaffected, or at least affected very little, by the darkness.

Three belonging to children, and three to adults.

Three members of the Pretty Boy Detective Club, and three members of the Twenties.

No one else was present—there was no trap, at least as far as I could see.

I don't know exactly how Rei integrated the information she got from me and the information she got from the guy on the phone, or how she analyzed it once she had, but she paused for a moment at the top of the stairs.

"Sotoin," she said over her shoulder, "you open the

door."

"So I shall," he answered pompously, and sure enough, he reached for the knob. I suppose the principle of ladies first is always beautiful, whether the lady in question is good or bad.

And then—

30. The Seed of Defeat

Suddenly, something pounded me on the crown of my head.

Or that's what I thought, the light was so intense—I didn't have the slightest notion what was happening, but my eyes are so excessively good that as long as I've taken off my glasses, or they've been taken off of me, even the strongest glare won't blind them. I can be in total darkness or brilliant light, and still my range of vision is the same.

I quickly realized what was going on.

A searchlight was sweeping over me.

Not just me, either, but all four of us—or to be more specific, a violently overpowering beam of light was shining down from above onto Rei.

"..."

Rei, who unlike me had only average eyesight, squinted up at it—and only after putting on her sunglasses with one hand did she realize she wasn't looking at a UFO in search of human specimens, but at a helicopter.

In contrast to the helicopter I'd ridden in the night before, this was a stealth helicopter whose propeller didn't make the usual racket. Because of the angle, I couldn't read the entire phrase printed on the body, but I was able to make out the last two words—Prefectural Police.

"Whew, that's a bit too bright of a spotlight to welcome my arrival. Even I might get washed out by that thing," Sotoin babbled on as he closed the door. His words were idiotic, but in fact, he was exploiting the fact that he had hold of the doorknob to casually close off Rei's escape route.

I lowered my gaze and looked straight ahead.

The six figures I'd made out from the other side of the steel door were indeed standing there, including three members of the Pretty Boy Detective Club—Nagahiro Sakiguchi, Michiru Fukuroi, and Sosaku Yubiwa.

Nagahiro the Orator, Michiru the Epicure, and Sosaku the Artiste.

We'd only been apart for a few hours, but it felt like ages—and our reunion felt like a miracle.

I couldn't believe I was getting so emotional—but a less abstract surprise was right before my eyes.

The three hostages.

13, 18, and 19, the captured members of the Twenties.

Were nowhere to be seen.

Not that I knew what every member of the Twenties

looked like—but *none of the three adults* on the roof looked like the sketches that Yubiwa had drawn from Mr. Bare-Legs' and my descriptions.

Since the Pretty Boys had based their hunt for the people who had been following me on those sketches, it would be unnatural for not one of the three hostages to match the images—but none of them did.

And they weren't tied up.

Which is to say, their clothes were casual, but their truncheon-at-the-ready stances made it obvious they were police.

"So they don't just have a criminal in the club, one of them's buddy-buddy with the cops, too, I see," Rei muttered, still holding me close.

At first, I didn't understand what she was saying, her mind moved so much faster than mine—but I was sure she must be surprised that they hadn't merely called the police, they'd gotten their full cooperation.

On second thought, maybe not.

My own reaction aside, something like that wouldn't surprise Rei—she'd known the hostage exchange was likely to be a trap from the start.

Essentially, nothing would have surprised her.

She was mentally prepared—and being mentally prepared, she shouldn't have fallen into the trap, no matter what it was. And yet.

"...Hnh."

She threw the cell phone on the ground with a clatter.

"I suppose you were the one I was talking to this whole time?" she asked, looking straight ahead without a glance at the discarded phone.

The person who stood there before her was the student council president.

Nagahiro the Orator—he too pulled the cell phone he was holding away from his ear. It looked the same as the one Rei had thrown down—19's phone, probably.

"That's right, Boss," Sakiguchi replied.

This wasn't his usual voice-actor's voice—it was the voice of 19, which we'd heard in the limo. Which meant I'd never actually heard 19's voice—the whole time, I'd been listening to the student council president speak.

"I'm guessing you two don't just happen to have similar voices... Which means...you're a *vocal impersonator*?"

"That's right, Boss."

The words were the same, but this time the voice was Sakiguchi's—ah, what a lovely voice. By then, even a dullard like me could guess exactly what the vice president's plan had been.

The point of pretending he was one of the Twenties wasn't to convince Rei that the hostages were unharmed—it was to convince her, without coming right out and saying it, that *there was no trap on the roof*. The strategy rested on the strong trust between Rei and her team.

Vocal impersonation.

Nagahiro the Orator—the pretty boy with a thousand voices.

So he didn't just sound good—he could copy whatever voice he wanted? He acted like it was nothing, but that was a mind-blowing skill to possess.

Simply copying someone's voice wasn't enough.

There were vocal tics and nuances of speech to consider, along with word selection, emotion, and the relationship between conversation partners—even over the phone, impersonating someone else was no joke.

And this voice actor did it all without losing his composure—he crossed swords with an adult opponent.

"Rest assured, all three of your employees are unharmed. As I promised, they've been treated with the utmost courtesy—and right now I believe they are being questioned with all due respect for their civil rights."

"...I see," Rei nodded quietly.

For someone who'd fallen into a trap and was now surrounded, she didn't give any sign of defeat—and Sakiguchi, who'd just done a splendid job of nabbing a criminal, didn't reveal a glimmer of triumph or pride.

Of course not.

Rei literally had me by the scruff of the neck—and Sotoin and Mr. Bare-Legs were still well within her range.

The battle was far from over.

"Impressive, considering you didn't even discuss

your strategy beforehand—or tell me, Sotoin, did you orchestrate this? Is this your brand of leadership—that time on the phone, when you mentioned Chinese food, was it the code name for your strategy?"

"Not a bit of it."

Sotoin flatly rejected her overestimation of him.

I swear, this leader.

"I see. Then this must be your typical M.O. I can accept that… But Mayumi."

She pulled me even closer as she spoke—her voice growing abruptly serious.

"I was foolish enough to fall for their plan… But tell me, how did they fool you? Even if you couldn't tell they'd switched out the three hostages by looking at the fuzzy silhouettes on the other side of the steel door, with your eyes you must have realized there was a helicopter—"

"Come, come! You can't seriously be asking that question!" Sotoin interrupted, as if he was laughing off what could only be called a deadly serious question on her part. "Do you really have no idea what you did? This outcome was entirely inevitable for both you and this story."

"What do you mean?"

Rei, who was usually so good at guessing people's thoughts, sounded genuinely flummoxed—and so was I, even though I was the topic of discussion.

I knew why I hadn't been able to see through

Sakiguchi's phone ruse—my eyes can see, but they can't hear.

I have no way to detect a trap constructed from sound.

But the same can't be said for a helicopter, even a stealth helicopter.

Sakiguchi didn't weave this net around Rei with my eyes in mind—from his position, asking the reinforcements to hang back was simply the natural thing to do.

But no matter how much the helicopter hung back, it would have been within my field of vision.

It doesn't matter if it's a person shadowing me, someone lying in wait, or any other sort of trap—I'll detect it whether I like it or not. I become an unintentional witness to everything—so why didn't I see the helicopter hovering in the sky as it waited for Rei?

She and I turned together toward Sotoin, who was pointing straight up and smiling smugly despite still being a hostage.

He was pointing not at the helicopter but at the sky. The star-filled night sky—the sky I had spent ten pointless years gazing at.

"After all, it was you yourselves who deprived young Dojima of her desire to look up at the sky."

31. An Arresting Drama

Rei mumbled something to herself.

As I just mentioned, all my "talent" is concentrated in my eyes, so I didn't hear her very clearly, but I think she said, "I could probably handle a crowd this size, but oh well."

Huh…? What did that mean?

Before I could think it through, she unpeeled her arm from my shoulder—and after handing me back my glasses, she gave me a light push from behind as I stood there in confusion.

"You can go now."

Then she glanced back at Sotoin, and Mr. Bare-Legs on his back, and told them, "You too, go on and join your friends."

"We'll take you up on that," Sotoin replied, grabbing my hand since I was standing there like a statue, and pulling me over to Sakiguchi and the others—with the strength of a boy, girl's outfit not withstanding.

As if they were taking our places, the three adults who had been playing the role of the hostages—that is, the three police detectives—walked toward Rei. She held out her hands of her own accord, with no sign of resistance, as she was surrounded, handcuffed, and taken away.

As the detectives led her into the school, one of them turned back toward us.

"Take it easy, Michiru," he said.

He knew Fukuroi?

I looked at him questioningly.

"He's not exactly a 'friend,'" the bossman said, sounding irritated. "I owe old man Morisaka a couple of favors from way back—when I was a bad kid."

Wasn't he still a bad kid?

That reminded me, though, how earlier he'd been talking about the police like he knew all about them—anyway, it seemed the Pretty Boy Detective Club had a pipeline to the police, albeit a thin one.

Thanks to which, I'd narrowly escaped disaster.

No... The real reason might be that Rei had let me go. And not just me—the Pretty Boy Detectives, too.

Our age was our biggest weapon after all.

Though that was kind of hard to accept.

After watching the helicopter disappear into the night sky, Sotoin turned to the other members of the club.

"Good work, lads. I suspect this incident will go down in history as yet another glorious and beautiful adventure of the Pretty Boy Detective Club," he declared ostentatiously—for some reason, the guy who just got rescued sounded the proudest of them all.

"Though the real adventure starts now, of course… They're sure to rake us over the coals down at the police station. Dear oh dear, I wonder how much we should tell them…" By contrast, Sakiguchi sounded troubled.

Which made sense.

Rei had let me go, but that didn't mean anything was resolved—the reality of what I had witnessed hadn't disappeared.

Still, I could easily imagine the uproar that would take place if we told the police the truth—we had a mountain of very real problems to take care of.

Given everything that had happened since morning, I doubted our enemies would make another move right away—but Sakiguchi, Fukuroi, and Yubiwa still looked glum.

"Before we worry about that…" Mr. Bare-Legs murmured sluggishly from Sotoin's back. He'd woken up, but he still looked worn out. "Is there anything to eat around here? I'm starving."

"…There sure is. Your favorite, Chinese food, and plenty of it," Fukuroi—that is, Michiru the Epicure—replied.

No one does it like the Pretty Boy Detective Club cook.

He'd made what the leader ordered—which I be-latedly realized he intended as a reward for Mr. Bare-Legs, who'd used up more of his energy than any of them.

The leader didn't do any deducing, and he didn't do much else, either—but he did seem qualified to lead, in a different way than Rei.

"Dojima. You can have some too, if you promise to swallow it all like a normal person."

I may be an incorrigible contrarian, but I couldn't resist Fukuroi's invitation, so I nodded eagerly and said, "Yes please!"

The mountain of problems was still—no.

I'm done with that kind of thinking.

32. Epilogue

After school the next day, I was walking down a little-used hallway on my way to the art room when I saw an extremely sexy female teacher standing in front of me—although given the plunging back of her outfit, excessively might be a better word than extremely. I was wondering if we'd always had such an outrageously beautiful teacher at our school when I looked a bit closer and realized it was Rei.

Rei?!

"Don't act so surprised—jailbreaks are kind of a hobby for me."

Sure, just drop that into conversation with a straight face.

"The police had three of my dear team members locked up, you know—I simply had to rescue them."

"..."

As usual, she answered all my questions before I even asked them.

I realized that she hadn't let us all go just because we

were kids and she was a softie at heart—although considering she'd let herself be captured for the sake of her team, albeit temporarily, maybe she was kind of a softie after all.

Either way, if she could answer my questions before I even asked them, she probably knew what I was thinking at that moment, too—which was, *Why had she put on a costume and broken into my school?*

The costume itself was on par with the work of the Pretty Boy Detective Club's costume artist—

"Work, of course. Just doing my job."

When she said that, I tensed in preparation for an attack.

But was it pointless? If she was here to kidnap me again, on the heels of my kidnapping the day before, I had no way to prevent it—

"Not that kind of work. I'm delivering something—and today, you're on the receiving end."

"D-Delivering… something?" I finally managed to respond.

"Yes. A message for you."

She calmly approached me.

"It's from the people who asked me to kidnap you yesterday… Oh, don't get nervous. They want to avoid a fuss more than anyone—they withdrew that commission after my failed attempt yesterday."

" … "

I wasn't sure if I could believe her—although when I

thought about it rationally, I realized my concern didn't exactly make sense, since we were the ones who fooled *her* the day before.

"Instead, they have a deal to offer you—since they've been monitoring you for ten years, of course they know your dream is to become an astronaut—and as you may have guessed, they exert quite a bit of influence over the development of this country's space program. Though not as much as JAXA, of course," she added, sniggering.

Apparently, she found my timid response hilarious.

Or maybe the content of the message was unbearably amusing?

"Sure… I figured as much, but… what about it?"

"Like I said, they have a deal for you—and unlike the trap Mr. Lolicon laid for me, this is an honest business deal with no tricks on either side. If you agree to keep your mouth shut about what you saw ten years ago, they say they'll help you get where you want to go."

"Help me… ?"

"In other words, I believe they mean they'll make sure you become an astronaut."

She was still smirking.

"Perhaps I should be congratulating you—with this, those ten years, those ten lonely years you spent stargazing, won't have been for nothing. To the contrary, it seems they were the shortest possible route to becoming an astronaut. The best possible cost performance to get you into space—the star you wanted to find may not exist, but you should at least be able to land on Mars. Of course, you'll need to take good care of your eyes, but I think they decided that given what you know, it makes the most sense to bring you into the family. If you were to say—"

"No thank you."

"Right, if you were to say no thanks—what?"

Rei's smile vanished, and her serious expression returned—which felt good, like I was finally getting in a shot after everything she'd done to me since the day before.

"You're turning them down? …I mean, if that's what you want, that's what I'll tell them—but you must realize that life doesn't offer many opportunities this good, that is, deals this good. And if a criminal like me is saying that, you know it's true. You might as well take full advantage of it, even if it is part of their scheme. Your future is hanging in the balance, so maybe you shouldn't make up your mind so quickly."

My future is hanging in the balance?

So what?

I know a guy who said what I was about to say when his *life* was hanging in the balance.

"That's not a beautiful way to live."

Rei gaped at me for a second, but as you'd expect from such a capable woman, she quickly seemed to switch mental channels and said, "I see," reviving her bewitching smile.

"Don't worry, I don't plan to tell anyone else about what I saw ten years ago—the Pretty Boy Detective Club swears their clients to secrecy, you know."

"I see. I'll pass that along."

She started walking away down the hall, as if to say there was no point in hanging around any longer—but then glanced back like she'd just remembered something.

"Oh, Mayumi, I almost forgot to ask. Do you always dress like that?"

"Huh? Oh, um…"

"It suits you—I mean, I'm not one to interfere with anyone's personal fashion choices, but it does look our relationship is going to be a long one."

With that, the boss of the criminal organization known as the Twenties strutted off down the hallway of my school with an assertive but also boundlessly elegant step, like a model on a runway.

… A long relationship?

That was the polar opposite of what she'd said the day before, but what did she mean? If she had been sharp enough to figure out what I was planning to do next from my facial expression alone, then nothing could've been more ominously unsettling.

That said, I couldn't stand in the hallway forever—so I started off toward the art room again.

The art room that was more like an art museum.

The headquarters of the Pretty Boy Detective Club.

"How do you do!"

I had no idea what to say when I opened the door, so I somehow ended up with this weird greeting—and once again, I found myself the target of suspicious looks from the boys inside.

So embarrassing… But something stiff and formal like "pardon me" didn't seem quite right at this point.

Anyway, my weird greeting wasn't the only reason they were staring at me.

"What's that about?" asked Michiru the Epicure, aka Michiru Fukuroi, who was in the middle of pouring tea for the other club members. He sounded openly irritated.

"Hell of a one-eighty. What are you, one of those people who bullies their coworker into quitting and then, when they do quit, criticizes them because quitting is irresponsible?"

Boy oh boy oh boy.

The satire was out in full force.

"Personally, I prefer girls in skirts. But since everyone wears black stockings anyway, it doesn't really matter, does it?" remarked Hyota the Adonis, aka Mr. Bare-Legs, aka Hyota Ashikaga, as he sat upside-down on the sofa swinging his exposed legs. The exhaustion from the day before seemed to be completely gone.

"Well, I'm in favor of it. That wig looks entirely natural, and overall I'd say she's very elegant," Nagahiro the

Orator, aka Sakiguchi, put in generously, in that lovely voice of his.

With his combination of ingenuity and craftiness, he had probably contributed the most to the events of the previous day by taking Rei down, but apparently even he couldn't tell that I wasn't wearing a wig. Maybe he just wasn't interested in girls' hairstyles past a certain age— but in a sense, this bobbed cut was my way of settling things with those parents of mine I was always arguing with.

As usual, Sosaku the Artiste, aka Sosaku Yubiwa, didn't say anything—but if I was to take a page from Rei's book and read his face, I think maybe he was dissatisfied with the low level of perfection? It was true that since he never did teach me how to apply the makeup and everything, I'd been forced to copy him based on memory— and matching the achievement of a genius is no easy task.

"Dojima. Why are you still wearing a disguise? Did you get hooked on that pretty boy look or something?"

I had indeed.

I was done up exactly like I had been the day before when we were trying to throw off the people who were following me—although the phrase "exactly like" might offend the child genius.

I'd cut my own hair, so I couldn't really say I looked the same—but, why had I done it? It was hard to explain.

It's not that I didn't know the answer—I did—but

coming out with it was tough. That had less to do with my contrary nature and more to do with plain old embarrassment.

To cover up my feelings, I looked around the art room—and noticed the all-important leader was missing.

"Where's Sotoin?"

"Hmm? Oh, like I said, it's elementary. He can't get here right after classes end."

Sakiguchi seemed to be implying he'd explained all this to me before—and I did remember him saying something similar, but I didn't really understand what he meant.

What was so elementary about it?

Also, now that my case had been at least temporarily resolved, some more fundamental questions were surfacing—questions about Manabu Sotoin.

Setting aside his good looks, why would such a conspicuous oddball not have the sort of reputation around school that the other club members did?

…Was he even a student at our school?

But, he definitely wore a Yubiwa Academy uniform…

"Um, Sakiguchi? Sorry about the abrupt question, but what year and class is Sotoin in?"

"Year 5, class A," he answered immediately.

For an instant, I wondered if he meant year five in the European sense, which would be the same as the second year of high school. It would make sense for me to not know a high school student, and Yubiwa Academy High School did have the same uniforms as us. But this was Japan, not Europe.

If he said year five, that would have to mean year five of elementary school.

"What?! Wait, that's why you're always saying it's 'elementary'? That's what you meant?!"

"That's right. Yubiwa Academy has an elementary school with the same uniforms, does it not?"

Sakiguchi and the other members tilted their heads quizzically, as if they couldn't figure out what I was fussing about after all this time, but of course I couldn't overlook this revelation, and was about to ask another question, when—

"Ha ha ha!"

The door of the art room flew open to the sound of loud laughter. It was Manabu the Aesthete, aka Manabu Sotoin, president of the Pretty Boy Detective Club—who had just walked over from the elementary school after classes ended.

Was it proper to walk in while laughing...?

"Sorry I'm late, lads! And what have we here? Who could this be? Well, if it isn't young Dojima—my, your eyes do look beautiful today!"

"..."

Zero to raucous in under two seconds.

While he didn't mention my outfit at all, he brought

up my eyes yet again, knowing full well how sensitive I was about them—but oddly enough, for once I didn't get mad.

Partly, it was because I had other things on my mind.

It was true that he was smaller than me, and now that I'd been told he was a fifth grader, I could see how he looked like one—and his ignorance about astronomy and flat-out statements about his own lack of knowledge all made sense if he was in elementary school.

He acted childish because he actually was a child.

He was the most boyish boy of them all.

The little brother of the club—was its president.

But I wasn't fully satisfied with that explanation—and of course, I still had heaps of questions. Why was a fifth grader coming over to the middle school every day after school to hang out? Was this elementary school kid really able to command a bunch of famous middle school students? How did the club come to exist? How had he gathered this group of wildly eccentric pretty boys? And class A? Really? But I swallowed all those doubts.

Now wasn't the time to ask questions—it was the time to say what I wanted to say.

I'd already decided on the words I would use when I saw Sotoin.

And—I'd dressed for the part.

"Hey, Sotoin. You said you're always recruiting new members, right? Well, would you let me join the Pretty Boy Detective Club?"

"Ha ha ha! What can I say? You know I can't turn down a request like that!"

…When consent comes that readily, the person who screwed up her courage to ask is the one who doesn't know what to say. Actually, though, Sotoin's response felt more like a rash decision than ready consent—and I definitely did know he was that kind of guy.

"What the hell?! Are you crazy, Dojima?!"

I was actually grateful for Fukuroi's reaction. My request seemed to have taken the other three by surprise, too—and while I must admit that it's an expression of my lousy personality in the worst possible taste, I did find it satisfying to see the school celebrities get flustered.

"But the question is, why? What changed? As far as I knew, you wanted to become an astronaut, no?"

Sotoin was the only one who stayed calm, but as the club's leader, he voiced the feelings of its members—that was what made him Manabu the Aesthete.

"I thought you of all people would be able to help me find a way to use my eyes—that unlike Rei, you'd use them in the service of good. No, not good… Beauty."

"Hmm. It seems you too have fallen captive to beauty after all. I knew from the start that this would happen!"

Just like a famous detective claiming after the case is solved that he knew who the villain was all along, Sotoin proudly puffed out his chest—but now that he mentioned it, I remembered he really had said something like that.

Not that I felt like I'd lost to him.

I'm done competing over things like that.

"How to use your eyes, eh? I ought to tell you to buck up and figure that out for yourself, but sadly my aesthetic won't let me do that. Alright! A beautiful aesthetic is about teaching as well as learning."

"Hey, are you crazy? Hellooo, she's a girl?" Fukuroi was almost coming out of his seat.

"If she has a boy's heart, I don't see the problem," Sotoin said to pacify him. "It's not as if you boys had to pass some test to get in. If she's got the odd notion in her head that she wants to join our group, then that's qualification enough. What's more, Kobayashi is naturally the first of Kogoro Akechi's assistants to come to mind, but we must never forget that he also had an assistant named Mayumi, who was herself a girl—if we ignored this sign, we could hardly call ourselves detectives, now, could we."

Wow, I didn't know that either.

And I wasn't sure how I felt about being chosen because of my name...

Still—assistant to a great detective?

Not bad.

"Michiru, start cooking for a welcome party right away. Show the new recruit the value of your presence in this organization. Everyone else, prepare for the celebration. Nagahiro, the welcome speech is in your hands. Hyota, I'm very much looking forward to your tap dance.

And Sosaku, how about taking this opportunity to make membership badges for everyone? The design is entirely up to you. You have my permission to go all out on this occasion."

The president's unilateral decision-making definitely crossed the line from self-importance into tyranny, but no one uttered another word of complaint—they all simply got to work as if they might as well accept it.

Sotoin turned to me.

"Allow me to welcome you, young Mayumi Dojima. Your tumultuous birthday has passed, but still you've failed to become an adult. Rest on your oars here as long as you like, until a new dream presents itself, until you desire once more to look up at the sky. I'm certain one day you'll find another star that shines down brightly upon you. Search well for that star, for searching is our duty. Welcome to the Pretty Boy Detective Club."

He held out his right hand.

"Let us be pretty, let us be boys, let us be detectives."

"And let's be the best team there is."

I took his hand and squeezed it hard. As ardently as a hug.

And so, on the first day of my life as a fourteen-year-old, I gave up my dream—a little proudly, and just a little bit beautifully.

Afterword

Children are often made to write about their dreams for the future, but I don't think many would do that sort of thing spontaneously if they weren't literally made to. And when they're made to write such things, they inevitably have to cement some kind of vision for themselves, such as, "When I grow up, I want to be a blah blah blah," or, "In the future, I'd like to blah blah blah," which seems to me to require quite a high level of skill. But our society clings so strongly to the idea that children without a dream for the future are "unhealthy" that most of them grudgingly choose from among a set of known options, selecting some flashy or highly profitable or otherwise superficially enticing job, so that it's no surprise most of these dreams never come true. I believe this has less to do with the harshness of life in the big wide world than it does with the fact that as children learn more, their options expand, and they realize they can do something else if they want to. In the end, our present-day self is the one who thinks about our future dreams and future self, and the future can't be decided unless we first do something about our present situation. Personally, I don't think there's any need for children to narrow their dreams for the future down to a single choice—they might as well write down every job they can think of. If any one of them pans out, then it's a dream come true. Do I mean that there's more than one path to one's dreams, and more than one destination? Well, since everyone starts looking for their next dream as soon as the last one is fulfilled, it doesn't make much difference if you achieve them in sequence or in parallel, does it? If having one big dream is praiseworthy, isn't having lots of little ones equally praiseworthy?

And so we arrive at this new series. I thought quite a lot about what to write in this volume, the first in a new series from a new imprint, and how to make this book different from those in the Kodansha BOX and Kodansha Novels lines, but in the end I decided the most important thing was that I write the book spontaneously, and the result is what you've just read. My sense is that it did come out differently from books in those other lines, though, so I suppose everything turned out alright in the end. And that's the story of *Pretty Boy Detective Club: The Dark Star that Shines for You Alone*.

The cover art and illustrations of the beautiful members of the Pretty Boy Detective Club were kindly drawn for us by Kinako. Thank you so very much! And over at the Third Literature Department, I look forward to working with the staff of Kodansha Taiga just as I have with the people at Kodansha Novels and Kodansha BOX.

NISIOISIN

MAYUMI DOJIMA

Prolific and palindromic NISIOISIN won the 2002 Mephisto Prize at the age of only twenty for his debut mystery novel *Decapitation: Kubikiri Cycle*. Since then he has penned more than one hundred novels across numerous series, in addition to many comics and television scripts. He is one of the best-selling Japanese authors in recent memory, and has been hailed for breaking down the barriers between mainstream literary fiction and so-called light novels.